MOMENTS OF DISARRAY

An Alex Kennedy Story

MEGAN HART

Copyright © 2018 by Megan Hart

All rights reserved. By purchasing this book, you have been granted the non-exclusive, non-transferable right to access and read the text of this book. No part of this text may be reproduced, transmitted, downloaded, decompiled, reverse engineered, or stored in or introduced into any information storage and retrieval system, in any form or by any means, whether electronic or mechanical, now known or hereinafter invented, without the express written permission of the publisher.

This is a work of fiction. Names, characters, places and incidents are the product of the author's imagination and are fictitiously. Any resemblance to actual persons, living or dead, business establishments, events or locales is entirely coincidental.

ISBN:**978-1-940078-49-6**

For everyone who asked for more Alex, thank you for letting me share more of his story.

To Lori Meckley for giving this bad boy a beta read. I appreciate it so much!

To my copyeditor, REB. Thanks for making my words better.

Keeping me humble…

Blurb

Alex Kennedy knows he's a rascal. A rogue. An arrogant bastard. He wreaked havoc on his best friend's marriage by falling in love with his best friend's wife, and now he's trying to move on. Sex, drugs, booze, boys, girls and toys. He's hell-bent on forgetting the past and running toward a future he doesn't believe he deserves, only to discover the truth in moments of disarray.

This novella takes place after Tempted and Everything Changes but before Naked. It includes an alternate version of the events Alex talks about in Vanilla.

Chapter 1

Sometimes, as the song said, love just ain't enough.

If anyone had told Alex Kennedy four months ago that he'd have ended up fucking his best friend's wife, he might've grinned, maybe even made a little bow and a flourish. Like he was proud of himself. If someone had said he would fall in love with Anne Kinney, drown in her, as a matter of fact, he'd have laughed out loud. Laughed so hard he'd cry.

But he had fucked her, and he did love her, and the weight of all of that had made him small and tired and bruised. He ached with it, tossing and turning, unable to sleep. Food tasted sour; he couldn't eat. The best he could do was try to wash away the taste of her with whiskey or gin or cheap draft beer in bars where people line danced and men in trucker caps and roping boots sometimes let him take them home.

"I'm not…I mean I never," said the one sitting on the bed next to him. Drunk, red-faced, but with a body like it had been carved out of fucking brick. His jeans bulged with an erection that belied any hesitation.

Alex shrugged, already unbuttoning his shirt. "Okay."

He stripped out of his clothes, knowing the other guy was watching, and, naked except for his briefs, went to the dresser where he'd already filled two glasses with ice. He poured them each a couple shots of Jameson from the bottle he'd picked up earlier today — Pennsylvania was fucking crazy with its liquor laws, and he'd had to go without for a couple days until he could find a liquor store in downtown Philly. Not like Ohio, where you could get drive-thru beer and wine in the drugstore. The first burn of the whiskey was sweet. The second, a little numbing. Heat spread down his throat into his belly as he turned, glass in hand.

"Here."

He pressed the glass into the other guy's hand. Kent, that was his name. Or maybe it was Brent. Or Trent. Alex didn't care. Whatever his name was, he was blond and tall and built like a Norse god, and by the looks of the bulge in his pants, he had a ten-inch cock.

Alex didn't sit next to him. He stood, sipping barely chilled liquor, and watched him. The guy — Luke, that was his name. Not Kent or Brent or Trent. Luke took the glass and tipped it to his lips, and he didn't cut his gaze away from Alex's. His tongue came out to press the small dent in his lower lip. He might have "never," but he sure as fuck looked like he knew what he was doing.

The burn of desire in Alex's belly had been kindled in the bar but cooled during this random happenstance of a courtship. Fucking men who claimed they were straight could be fun, sexy, a challenge. Tonight it seemed like it was just going to be a lot of work, more than Alex wanted to take on. And that was something new, wasn't it? That he'd pass up the chance to get off because it was too much effort?

"You can go," he said to Luke now. "If you want."

"No! I mean. No, that's not what I want."

Alex eyed him. The bulge in the other guy's briefs had not softened. If anything, the spreading damp spot on the fabric proved what he'd just said. Alex tossed back the rest of his drink and set the glass on the night stand. He curled a hand around the back of Luke's neck and leaned as though to kiss him.

"Yes, fuck, yes…please…" Luke groaned, his eyes closed. Mouth open.

That sound of complete consent, of utter desire, made Alex's cock twitch. "Yes, what?"

Luke opened his eyes. "Kiss me?"

"No," Alex told him. "How about you suck my cock, instead?"

The other man blinked rapidly. He slid his tongue along his lower lip. He didn't move away, but beneath Alex's hand, all the muscles of Luke's neck tensed.

"I don't know how," he whispered finally. "I told you. I've never done this before."

In answer, Alex unzipped his jeans and pushed them down over his hips. His cock thickened, pushing at the front of his briefs. He tugged down the waistband of the soft material, letting his dick spring free.

"Put your mouth on it," he said in a low voice, keeping it kind of gentle.

Luke shuddered and swallowed. The muscles of his throat rippled beneath that golden skin. Jesus, he was built like a fucking bull. Thick and muscled all through his shoulders and back. Thighs like tree trunks. Alex had never gone for guys who looked they could break him half, but Luke had a vulnerability that softened him. It didn't seem like a show, either, and Alex was usually good about smelling bullshit from a mile away.

"Just take it in slow," Alex murmured.

Luke scooted forward on the bed. He looked up at Alex, heat burning in his gaze, his mouth slightly open, lips wet. He licked them, and the sight of his tongue sent a shudder down Alex's spine that ended up centered at the base of his cock, which twitched again.

He put a hand on the back of Luke's neck, fingers curled. Not pushing. Guiding. Luke kissed the head of Alex's cock.

"Like that," Alex urged.

Luke moaned. Under Alex's touch, the other man's body tensed and released as he moved even closer. He took the head of Alex's cock, then, surprisingly, the rest of it all the way to the base. Sucked it, releasing it slowly. Alex's hips bucked forward even though he tried not to, trying not to choke the guy on his first time out.

Alex breathed out, a soft and low sigh of appreciation. "Fuck. That's good."

Luke moaned again, the sound a hum around the shaft of Alex's dick. He slid his mouth off it, then down again. Faster this time. Alex tried to twist his fingers into the bristle brush cut of Luke's hair, but it was too short to make purchase. He let his head fall back, eyes closed, as Luke sucked him a little harder.

"Good?" Luke mumbled with a mouthful of Alex's prick.

Alex laughed under his breath. "Yeah. It's good. Use your hand, stroke it while you suck. Yes, oh, fuck, fuck, yes. Like that."

Luke had reacted at once. Now his big hand engulfed Alex's cock, moving in time to the eager sucking action of his lips and tongue. Too eager, his teeth scraped at Alex's cock, but it was so hard now, so thick, that the pain caused no more than a small dip in the rising pleasure.

"Want you to come in my mouth," Luke managed to say.

Alex paused in the rolling of his hips. He focused through the haze of arousal to look down at the other guy. "You've thought about this a lot, huh?"

Luke released Alex's cock and swiped his tongue over his lips again. He looked as though he was going to reply, but instead only nodded. Then he cut his gaze, his expression twisting into shame, but he didn't try to move away.

"Hey." Alex waited until Luke looked up. "There's nothing wrong with wanting something."

Luke shifted on the bed a little bit, putting distance between his mouth and Alex's throbbing cock. "Maybe I should go."

Alex fisted his dick. "You could do that. If you really want. Is that what you really want, Luke?"

It was the first time he'd said the other guy's name aloud, and it clearly affected Luke, who shuddered and sighed out a gasping, breathy sort of moan. Still, he turned his face away and hung his head. His dick, which had been thrusting up from between those tree trunk thighs, even started to wilt a little.

What the hell was he doing, Alex thought. He should step aside and toss the guy his clothes. Don't let the door hit ya where the good lord split ya, as the saying went. He could finish himself off in the shower in five minutes and be asleep another five after that, and no fucking drama.

Instead, he sat on the bed next to Luke. Hips and thighs touching. He leaned against Luke, nuzzled his neck before withdrawing.

"There's nothing wrong," he repeated, "with wanting something."

Luke said nothing at first. They sat there for a minute or so. Breathing in, breathing out, and that was all.

Alex pushed Luke gently back, urging him to settle on the bed against the pillows. He snagged a condom from the nightstand drawer — he never forgot to stock his hotel room, and it was never for "just in case," because with Alex Kennedy there was *always* a reason to need a rubber. He slid it and the small bottle of lube beneath the pillow as he spooned behind the other man. Luke tensed, but didn't try to move away. After a few seconds, his trembling eased.

"I'm sorry," Luke said.

Alex huffed soft laughter. "Shhh."

His hand slipped around to take Luke's cock into his fist. Luke startled, but Alex didn't stop. Slow, slow, easy and light strokes, until Luke's cock was once again standing up proud. Alex closed his eyes, letting his own dick get hard against the smooth, thick muscles of Luke's ass and thighs.

"Tell me what you've thought about," Alex said in a low voice.

Luke sighed. "I…shit. I just want…I want…"

Alex didn't push for more. He pressed his teeth against Luke's bare shoulder. He rocked his hips slowly, nudging at Luke with his cock, letting the pleasure of that pressure fill him. With a small shift and a few seconds effort, he filled his palm with a dollop of lube. When he stroked it down Luke's prick, the other man cried out, wordless and hoarse.

He kept the pace steady. His grip, firm. Stroke, stroke, stroke, then a twist of his palm around the head of Luke's dick, then down again. A caress of the other man's balls. A stroke of a lubed finger along the sweet spot between Luke's balls and asshole, and then, lightly, a firm but gentle pressure there. When Luke moaned and pushed against that touch, Alex bit back a grin. Luke might not be able to tell him what he wanted with his voice, but his asshole sure was talking.

More lube. Another gentle probe of the tight ring of

muscles. Another series of twisting strokes up and down Luke's dick. A dewy glisten of precome formed at the tip of Luke's dick and slid down the shaft, mingling with the lube. The sight of it, yeah, fuck, that was hot.

Alex was usually the one getting his cock sucked or stroked, because that was how he liked it, but right now, here, something about Luke made him want to give the pleasure, not just take it. Maybe it was because he was a virgin, at least when it came to guys. Maybe it was something else, an idea of karma and payback. A way to make it up to the universe for the fuckery Alex had done. A good deed.

Luke had started pushing into Alex's grip. Alex slowed the stroking. He shifted, one leg pressing between Luke's, and shifted their bodies so Luke was more on his back with Alex on his side. He let his fingers press again at Luke's asshole, watching the other man's face. Nothing but desire there. He pressed a little harder, letting his fingertip ease inside. Luke made a wordless noise, but there was no way Alex was getting in there without some more lube, more preparation, and he sure as hell wasn't going to try to get in there without asking first.

"Here?" He pushed in again, not too deep, just barely breaching the ring of muscle. "Is this what you want?"

The other man didn't answer at first, but then said quietly, "I've used…things…when I'm jacking off. Yeah. I want that."

That was enough of an answer for Alex, surprised that Luke had admitted to assplay, although honestly not surprised the guy had done it. He lubed up again. Moved back into position. Luke's cock had softened, but that didn't matter right now. Alex's was hard enough for both of them.

He pushed his finger inside to the first knuckle. Then,

when Luke didn't protest, all the way in. Then out, slowly. Carefully, although as it turned out he didn't need to be as cautious as he'd expected. Luke's greedy little asshole had clearly seen some action before, because when Alex pressed in with a second finger, the other man opened for him.

"Like a fucking champ," Alex murmured.

Luke shuddered, groaning. His cock, limp on his thigh, leaked a steady stream of clear fluid. Alex slid two fingers inside him again, this time twisting, and could feel the growing knot of the other man's prostate. His own cock throbbed, knowing exactly how good that sweet pressure felt.

"Have you ever come this way?" he asked.

Luke shook his head. "No, no, just…I just tried a thing, but no, I didn't…"

Alex wondered what "a thing" was that Luke had stuck in his ass while jacking off, but now wasn't the time to find out. Anyway, did it matter? If there was going to be any judgement about Luke using something that wasn't meant to be a sex toy in his pursuit of getting off, it wasn't going to come from Alex.

"Do you want me to fuck you, Luke?" Luke didn't answer with words, and although the way he ground himself down on Alex's fingers seemed like agreement, it wasn't enough. Not for safety and not for Alex's ego, either. "You have to say it."

"I want you to fuck me," Luke said. "Please."

The "please," so pleading, so polite, sent a surge of desire through Alex's dick so strong he had to take a moment and breathe through it before he could withdraw his fingers and burrow beneath the pillow for the condom. It took him only a moment or so after that to tear it open, to sheathe himself, to add some lube. He pressed his rock hard dick against Luke's hole, pushing gently.

"I want it," Luke said and moved his body to push himself harder onto Alex's cock.

His dick went in suddenly, fast enough to make them both cry out. Alex gripped Luke's hip, not moving, but Luke was already rocking his hips to get that hard length deeper inside him. He shook with his pleasure, muttering pleas over and over. His cock slapped his thigh until Alex reached around to grip it. Then Luke fucked into Alex's grip.

Alex had thought to take this slow and easy, but Luke clearly couldn't hold off. It was clear he was new to this, rocking so fiercely he almost pulled Alex's cock out of him, but it was also easy to see that he was not in complete control, and that was hot enough to bring Alex close to the edge faster than he'd expected.

He fucked deeper, find that perfect rhythm. Making it work. Getting there, but not alone, making sure Luke was getting there, too. Their bodies slapped. The pillow shifted, bunching, and Alex yanked it out of the way. Luke strained and arched, writhing now, his cock leaking a continuous stream of precome that was started to tinge a creamy white. Alex was holding off only because he wanted to make sure the other guy came first — a matter of pride, to not leave Luke in the lurch. Not this, his first time.

"I'm gonna come."

Luke panted the words, ending on a strangled groan. His cock, still only half-hard, fountained creamy white fluid, not in jets, but a constant surging waterfall…the way you came from ass play, and the sight of that sent Alex spinning and falling into his own fierce climax. It was short, sharp and brilliant, and for those few glorious seconds, the world stopped turning and there was only this, only pleasure, nothing else but that, and as the sublime oblivion overtook him, Alex thought he could make it through at least one more day.

Chapter 2

Alex had not asked Luke to spend the night. Luke hadn't asked if he could stay and had headed out without fanfare. So when a knock came at the hotel room door at just past eleven the next morning, and a bleary eyed and bed-headed Alex looked through the peephole, the very last fucking thing he expected to see was the man whose cherry he'd popped the night before.

"Shit," Alex muttered and rested his forehead against the door.

This wouldn't be the first time he'd gained an admirer after what should have been a simple one-night stand, but he'd thought Luke knew the drill. Certainly the guy had been eager enough to fuck off out of there the night before without so much as a "can we cuddle?" moment, something for which Alex was grateful.

Another knock came, and Alex groaned. He opened the door a crack, well-aware he wore only a pair of low slung jeans, no shirt, his feet bare. He was showered, but barely. He'd had coffee, but again, only what could be considered coffee by the narrowest of margins, as it had come from the hotel room's shitty coffee maker. He was probably going to die of some mold-related disease.

"Hey." In one hand, Luke held up a white paper bakery bag dotted with grease and a small cardboard tray holding two large insulated cups in the other.

Alex opened the door and stepped aside to let him in, offering the way with a small gesture. He closed the door behind Luke. "Hey."

Luke set the drinks and bag on the small desk that this hotel had decided made this room a "business suite." Today he wore a pair of faded jeans, a black-and-red flannel shirt over a black Henley, and black boots. Blond bristles stood out on his chin and cheeks, and his eyes looked a little red. Like maybe he hadn't had enough sleep, Alex thought with a small internal grin he didn't show — he didn't want Luke getting the wrong idea about anything.

"I know you said last night that the worst part of living in a hotel was having to run out for coffee or order room service, so I figured you might like this," Luke said.

Alex's eyebrows rose. "I said that?"

"Yeah. At The Rusty Nail." Luke coughed into his fist. "Before you asked me if I wanted to come home with you."

"Ah, man, the night's a little blurry to be honest. I'll gladly take that coffee, though." Alex held out a hand. Luke pressed a hot cup into it, and Alex tipped it to his mouth with a grateful sigh.

"I have cream and sugar, if you want it."

"Nah. This is good." Alex sipped again. "Look, about last night…"

"I get it," Luke cut in. "I'm not trying to…umm…I mean, look, I didn't come here to get laid again."

Alex sipped coffee again. Gestured at the bakery bag

but said nothing. Luke opened it, pulled out a chocolate croissant and held it up with a questioning expression. Alex nodded, and it passed into his hand the way the coffee had.

"Thanks," he said. "I was starving."

Luke cleared his throat again. "I just thought you might like some breakfast."

"How do you know I didn't have some already? Or that I'd be here?"

Luke laughed, and fuck-a-doodle-doo, there was a set of dimples on each side of his mouth. Alex no longer had to wonder what had prompted him to take this guy home. The evidence was right there. Dimples.

"You also said that you were not a morning person and that you liked chocolate croissants, because we passed the bakery on the way back here. You don't remember any of this?"

"Not so much." Alex shrugged and took a bite of the croissant. Ahhh. Sugar. Caffeine. He eyed Luke as he chewed. The guy looked antsy.

Shit. Was there going to be some kind of declaration? A confession? It was too damned early for drama. It was always too early for that.

"Okay," was all Luke said. He pried the other cup out of the paper tray and drank it too fast, wincing and muttering "ouch" as he burned his mouth.

Alex said wryly, "Careful."

"Do you have plans for today?" Luke asked suddenly. Bluntly.

Alex considered this, taking his time in answering by looking around the room. Sipping some coffee. He took another small bite of the croissant and washed it down with more coffee.

"I was hoping I could just hang out with you today," Luke said before Alex decided how he wanted to answer.

Alex sighed. "Look, man…I don't think that's a great idea."

"It's a terrible idea," Luke agreed.

"So…why do you want to do it, then?" Intrigued, Alex looked him over.

Luke shrugged. Obviously there was a lot more going on under that blond hair, but he wasn't going to let it out. He looked Alex in the eye, though, and his gaze was straightforward and open.

Alex had nothing on his agenda for the day other than sending some emails to follow up on a few consulting gigs that had come his way. He owed some replies to stateside friends he'd promised he'd contact when he got here from being overseas, and although he'd been here for a while, he hadn't yet managed. He owed Jamie at least a phone call, which he'd been putting off and still didn't want to make.

"Sure. Okay. Let's hang out," he said.

Luke's smile looked relieved. "Great."

Chapter 3

"So...that's the Liberty Bell." Alex chuckled with a shake of his head. They'd waited in line for half an hour to see it, looked at it for two minutes, then moved on.

Luke grinned. "Yep. That was it."

"Thanks for taking me to see it, I guess." Alex shoved a hand in his jeans pocket as they left the building in which the bell was housed. "I was expecting something a little more impressive, not going to lie."

"Ain't that the way, though? Everything you wait so long for ends up being kind of underwhelming. Kind of like cheesesteaks."

Alex gave Luke a sideways glance. "You shut your whore mouth. Cheesesteaks are awesome."

Luke laughed after a startled look, probably at Alex's choice of admonition. "Oh, yeah, but around here, people act like Geno's and Pat's are the only place to get one. Truth is, I can take you to a place with a cheesesteak so good it will practically make you..."

"Cream my jeans?" Alex prompted when Luke didn't finish his sentence.

Luke laughed again, this time uncomfortably. "Something like that."

"Not a fan of coming in my pants, to be honest. Kind of messy." Alex turned around to walk a few steps backward while watching Luke's face carefully for a reaction.

They'd spent the afternoon sightseeing, and Luke had never once so much as made the effort to flirt. Didn't try to take Alex's hand, not that he was much for hand holding. No innuendos. His last comment had sounded offhanded, not something meant to get a rise out of Alex. It was curiouser and curiouser, as that little freak Alice was fond of saying.

"Luke!"

The male voice from behind them turned Alex in that direction. Luke turned too, his shoulders going stiff and straight. His jaw clenched and set.

"Hey, buddy." The man jogging up to them was a real bro. Long basketball shorts, a sleeveless tank, backwards baseball cap. He clapped Luke on the shoulder and rounded on Alex with a hand out. "Hey. Brent. I'm Luke's brother."

"Fraternity, not sibling," Luke said. "This is Alex."

"Alex, nice to meetcha." Brent pumped Alex's hand several times before dropping it.

He shifted from foot to foot in the way runners did at stop lights, so they didn't lose their momentum or whatever the fuck. Alex never ran, so he had no idea why they did that. Alex took a step back.

"Hey," he said.

"What are you up to, man?" Brent asked Luke.

"Ahh….just, umm, just showing Alex around the city."

Brent grinned, still jogging in place. "You from out of town, huh?"

"Yeah," Alex answered smoothly.

"Cool, cool. Hey, get him to take you to Pat's, King of Steaks, man. Don't let him try to take you to Geno's! Luke, see you later." Brent shook Alex's hand again, slapped Luke on the back hard enough to stagger him forward a step, then ran off.

Alex said nothing for a moment, but when he looked at Luke, he couldn't hold back the laughter. "Whoa."

"He's a good guy." Luke sounded a little defensive, but then he laughed, too.

"I'll tell you what, though, I could eat the fuck out of a cheesesteak."

Luke grinned. "Okay, but I told you, I'm not taking you to either one of those places. I've got a little dive bar favorite. I'll take you there. And…hey, thanks for not. You know."

"Dropping to my knees and blowing you right here in the middle of the street in front of your frat brother? No problem." Alex kept his tone neutral, an eye on Luke's expression.

Luke had the good grace to look a little ashamed, but he gave an honest answer. "Yeah. That."

"Don't worry about it. It's not like I was expecting you to take me home to meet your mom. We hooked up. Once." Alex held up a finger. He didn't point out that Luke had been the one to show up at his room this morning, that Luke had been the one to ask him to hang out.

"Brent wouldn't understand."

"Seriously," Alex said. "It's fine."

Luke shook his head. "It's not fine. It's a douche move on my part, to act like you're just some friend or something. Instead of, well…shit."

They were blocking the traffic on the sidewalk, and

Luke's voice had risen enough to attract attention. Alex didn't care much if the entire city of Philadelphia knew that he liked to get his dick sucked by other dudes, but somehow he didn't think Luke felt the same way. He gestured.

"Why don't you take me to this dive bar," he suggested.

Chapter 4

Alex had eaten cheesesteaks before, but the ones around home weren't like this. Soft hoagie roll, Cheese Whiz, thin sliced steak, onions. It was the Whiz that really got to him. It should've been disgusting, but he'd already devoured his entire sandwich and was eyeing the one Luke had ordered but had barely touched. He had, however, downed two pints of beer while Alex ate.

"I'm done." Alex pushed back from his plate with a sigh and stifled a belch. He'd had one beer to Luke's two, and was sticking more with water today. "Man, that was perfect. Thanks."

"Welcome."

Alex wiped his mouth with a paper napkin. They were almost the only ones in here, seated at the tiny two-top, so when he leaned forward he was pretty close to Luke's face. "So. You want to talk, or what?"

"Talk?"

"You showed up at my hotel room, specifically not asking for another round, which, you know, taken the wrong way could hurt a fella's feelings. You show me all around the city, which was a helluva nice thing to do for a stranger. You brought me here for a truly stellar sandwich. It's clear you want to talk to me about something, man. And look, I'm not much of an Agony Aunt, usually—"

"Agony Aunt?"

"Like an advice columnist," Alex explained. "I mean, normally, to be honest, I'm a 'live and let live' kind of motherfucker. Or maybe I'm a 'look out for number one' sort of guy. Whatever, I'm not the dude to come to when you need some sort of emotional support or anything like that. Usually."

"But you are today?"

Alex sat back with a small groan and rubbed his stomach. He wasn't about to explain everything about karma and his past to Luke. He barely wanted to think about it himself. "Let's just say you caught me at a weird time."

"Yeah. I guess you could say the same about me." Luke tossed back the rest of his beer and sighed.

"Are you going to eat that?"

Luke shook his head. Alex pulled the sandwich closer. He was probably going to regret eating it, but fuck that, he was probably going to regret this conversation.

"Last night changed my life," Luke said.

Alex finished the bite he was chewing. Swallowed. Washed his mouth clean with some water. A jokey comment rose to his lips, but something stopped him.

"Okay," was all he replied.

"Get you something else?" The craggy faced bartender had come over to grab their empty glasses.

"I think we're good." Alex grabbed for the check before Luke could take it, waving a hand at the other guy. "Dude. No. I got this."

Check paid, sandwich boxed up because it would make a delicious breakfast, Alex was leading Luke back to his hotel room so he could put the food in the minifridge. And also because he suspected that whatever was still percolating in Luke's innards was going to come out in a way that Luke would appreciate nobody else seeing. Luke had protested, just a little, at going back to Alex's room— but Alex was extremely persuasive when he wanted to be.

"Grab a seat." He didn't look at Luke as he popped the leftover box into the fridge. "Want a drink?"

"Just water. Do you have water?"

Alex handed him a bottle of water and took one for himself. He sat in the other chair, a good distance from Luke. "I knew when I was about ten."

"Knew?" Luke looked startled.

"Knew I was into guys. Also girls," Alex added. "But I was ten when I figured it out. I couldn't admit that for a long time. I told myself and other people, too, that I had other reasons for fucking guys. But the truth is, I always wanted to."

Luke leaned back in his chair and ran both hands through his hair. "I haven't figured out a damn thing! What's wrong with me?"

"Nothing's *wrong* with you. It's who you are. That's all. If you like guys, you just do." Alex couldn't keep the disgust out of his voice, but he did try to tone it down, and damn, look at him, being all kind and considerate and shit. He sent a silent two thumbs up to the universe, hoping he was going to get some points for all this. Knowing that in the end, it wouldn't matter. It couldn't change all the damage he'd done.

Luke let out a hitching breath that ended up sounding like a groan. "I don't want it to be who I am."

"You don't have a choice, man."

Luke looked at him. "If you like to be with women,

why don't you just…fuck, man. Why not just *be* with women?"

Alex had asked himself that question more than once, even a few times with that same measure of self-loathing that Luke had all over his face and in his voice. "Because it's not simple like that. Because I'm not straight. And by the way you sucked my cock last night, I'm going to say that you're not, either."

"Fuck you!" Luke stood. Water sloshed in the bottle he hadn't even cracked open.

Alex stood, too. "Isn't that what you want?"

He was only half-prepared for the swing Luke took at him, but the bigger guy seemed only half-trying to hit him. Alex stepped back in time to catch only a glancing hit to the jaw. It still hurt like fuck, but didn't lay him out. He had no doubts Luke could've done that if he wanted to, with half the effort he'd just made.

"Fuck you," Luke said again, this time in a whisper.

"The door is right there. All you have to do is walk out of it."

Luke looked over his shoulder, then back at Alex. In two steps, he was within reach. He grabbed Alex by the shoulders. Slanted his mouth across Alex's. Sloppy, no finesse, just desperation. Greed and need. Alex didn't move, didn't even put his hands up to hold onto Luke. He opened his mouth for the kiss. Luke pulled away, still gripping Alex by the shoulders.

"If you're going to hit me again," Alex said, "at least let me tell you my safe word."

Luke blinked rapidly. Took a step back, letting go. "I don't even know what that means."

"It doesn't mean anything. It was a joke."

"I'm a joke?"

Alex shook his head, wishing it wasn't so easy to fuck

up so hard with other people's feelings. "No, man. You're not a joke."

Luke's fists clenched. Released. Clenched again. Alex braced himself to duck out of the way of another swing, but Luke didn't try to hit him.

"I just don't know what to do," Luke said. "Everything is fucked up in my head. I shouldn't be here."

"But you are."

"I shouldn't have come here last night!"

"But you wanted to, and it sounds like something you wanted for a long time. And there's nothing wrong with what happened. We were safe," Alex added, thinking that might be a part of Luke's worry.

When the other man didn't say anything, Alex put his hands on Luke's waist, just above his hips. Luke was a much bigger man and Alex had to stretch a little to brush a kiss over his lips, hovering, breathing, letting Luke decide.

Luke kissed him again, this time with less fury. Their mouths eased apart. Alex licked his lips, letting his tongue flicker lightly along Luke's mouth, and the next kiss was deeper. When they pulled away from each other, Luke's gaze burned brightly to match the two high spots of color in his cheeks, but he seemed a little calmer.

"Why did you pick me up last night?" Luke asked.

Alex shrugged, not letting go of his waist. "I was drunk. You're hot. You looked interested. I'm indiscriminate."

"I don't know what that means," Luke said again, sounding defeated.

"It means I fuck a lot of guys."

Luke's brow furrowed. "But women, too?"

"Yes. I'm an equal opportunity slut." Alex laughed, but ruefully, the humor not enough to take away the sting of naming that truth.

"So, there wasn't something about me?"

Alex frowned. "Like what? Something special? If you're asking me if we had some kind of 'connection' — "

"No! I mean, no, that's not what I mean," Luke added quickly. "I just meant that I didn't seem like a fag."

"Don't," Alex replied coldly, "say it like that."

He pushed Luke a few steps back from him. This had been a mistake, fuck his life. And how could he be surprised? It's what he did, wasn't it? Let his dick rule his head. Make stupid choices. Try to do the right thing and fuck that all up, too.

"I'm sorry."

"I'm not interested in being your self-hating rationale," he told Luke flatly. "*I'm* not ashamed of who I am."

The lie was sweet instead of bitter. Poisoned sugar on his tongue. He *was* ashamed of who he was, but for a hundred thousand other reasons, not because he liked dick.

Luke didn't move toward him. He sank heavily onto the edge of the bed. "I'm sorry. I'm an asshole."

"Yeah. Kind of."

Luke lifted his chin. "You want to take a shot at me?"

"Oh, God. No." Alex shook his head and laughed, stepping back.

"I wouldn't blame you if you did."

Luke looked sincere. Apologetic. Big puppy eyes, paired with that bruiser of a body. He might not know how appealing he looked, but then again, Alex thought, he might.

"You looked like a straight frat boy who'd had just enough to drink to make him not care where the blowjob came from," Alex told him. "Considering we were in a country bar, I took a chance on getting a punch in the face or my dick sucked. Felt like it could go either way."

Luke considered this. "Has that ever happened to you?"

"I'm pretty fucking irresistible, so not usually. But yes. I've guessed wrong a few times."

"You weren't wrong about me," Luke said this in a voice so low Alex almost didn't hear him.

"Nope." Alex moved closer to nudge apart Luke's thighs so he could stand between them. He cupped the other man's face in his hands, tipping Luke's face upward.

Luke didn't say anything else.

Alex shrugged and moved away from him. "Like I said, there's the door."

Luke stood. "I guess I'll go."

When the other guy had reached the door, Alex said, "I don't ever have to beg to get laid. And I fucking hate feeling when someone expects sex to equal anything other than getting laid."

Luke paused without turning. "Yeah? So?"

"But I don't know anyone here, and I had a good time today," Alex said. "So if you want to hang out again, show me around, I've got business here for another week or two. Maybe longer. Maybe less."

Still without turning, Luke said, "Yeah, sure. That would be cool."

"Cool." Alex smiled, even though Luke couldn't see it.

"I've got some stuff I have to do tomorrow, and I have class on Monday, then work. But Tuesday I don't have class, and I have the day off."

"Tuesday, then," Alex said.

Chapter 5

If money couldn't buy happiness, it sure as hell could rent it for a while. Alex had cash in his pocket and a credit card with a spending limit so vast even he would have a hard time reaching it. Better than that, he had the money in his bank accounts to cover any debt he racked up. He'd worked hard enough to make it possible for him to never work again, or at least for a long time, but what exactly was he supposed to do if he didn't work?

He wasn't going to let himself think about his father, who'd often called him lazy, but there was no denying that not getting up before eleven if he didn't want to and spending all of Monday watching television hadn't done much to make Alex feel productive. But fuck the old man, he thought sourly. That asshole could work himself into the ground and never be close to the success Alex had made of himself. Too bad he didn't have anyone to share it with.

Again as it almost always did, his mind flashed to Jamie. And then of course, to Anne. It didn't matter that it was no good to think of her, to remember the taste of her kiss or the scent of her hair. It was no good to tell himself he'd done the right thing by leaving the way he had. None of it was good because *he* wasn't good, and he never would be.

When the knock came at his hotel room door, Alex considered not opening it. He'd made the invitation to Luke in a moment of weakness and truth — he had enjoyed the day with the younger man, and he didn't know anyone else in Philadelphia, not anyone he could count on to hang out with, anyway. But there'd been more there Alex did not want to think about, and sure as shit did not want to tell Luke. So he tossed around the idea of simply not answering the door, until the knock came again and he groaned under his breath at what an idiot he could be.

"Brought you coffee," Luke said when Alex opened the door. His grin broadened. "And chocolate croissants."

"You didn't have to. But thanks. C'mon in." Alex waved him inside and took the coffee and bakery bag.

"Are you into, like, weird stuff?"

The question surprised him. "You mean like getting tied up? Or tying someone up? Or something kinkier than that, like with feet or something?"

"Like with…feet…what the…?" Luke looked stunned. A crimson flush rose up his throat from where his unbuttoned flannel shirt showed his bare skin above the scooped neck of his t-shirt.

Alex laughed. "Not what you meant?"

"I don't think so, no. I meant like, are you into the world's biggest ball of twine or carnival side shows, that sort of weird stuff." Luke shook his head and sipped his own coffee. "Not umm…."

"Gotcha." Alex laughed again. "Sorry. I guess so? I mean, sure. Can't say I've ever been to a carnival sideshow. I didn't even know they still had things like that."

"I don't know if they do, to be honest."

Alex stared at the younger guy. "Are you always honest?"

"Umm…" Luke seemed taken aback, then abashed. "Nobody's always honest."

"That's the damned truth."

Luke frowned, but the expression smoothed after a moment or so. He moved closer to Alex. "I try to be as honest as I can, I guess. What about you?"

"Not me. I'm a Liar McLiarson. Pretty much every word out of my mouth is a lie," Alex said.

"So then you're lying about being a liar?"

"I guess you'll never know," Alex said. Being charming, because that's what he was good at.

Luke had a great laugh. Full bodied. It made Alex smile.

"I thought we could go check out the **Mütter Museum,**" Luke said. "It's got a plaster cast of the original Siamese twins, Chang and Eng."

"Whoa." Alex wasn't sure what to say about that, other than it sounded messed up. Fun, but messed up.

"If you don't want to, we don't have to," Luke said hastily. "I just thought —"

Alex stepped forward and kissed him.

Luke moaned lightly, his lips parting for the invasion of Alex's tongue. Alex pulled him closer, pressing their lower bodies together. Grinding a little. He was already getting hard. So was Luke. The meaty thickness of his cock nudged his jeans, and when Alex put a hand between them to cup the other man's groin, Luke pushed into the touch with a greedy, desperate sigh.

In the next moment, Luke dropped to his knees and tugged open Alex's button and zipper. He freed Alex's cock with a tug, pushing the denim over Alex's thighs. Luke took

Alex's dick deep into his mouth, no hesitation this time. The head of it nudged the back of Luke's throat, and it was Alex's turn to moan.

He hadn't expected this, not *exactly* this, but he wasn't going to turn it down. He put a hand on Luke's head, not guiding but encouraging. Luke might not have had much experience, but he made up for that with enthusiasm and generosity. He added a hand to the shaft, stroking as he sucked, the way Alex had told him to that first night.

It was good. Pleasure was the quickest way Alex had always found to force away any kind of thought — the bad and the good, but it was those dark thoughts he was interested in ignoring now. He let himself fall into the sensations of Luke's mouth and hand. He pushed forward into the wet, hot grip of Luke's lips and tongue, focusing on the building ecstasy.

Sometimes he could get off in minutes. Today it was taking longer. Luke, on purpose or without knowing it, was drawing out the blowjob by switching up the pace and rhythm, keeping Alex on the edge but never letting him go over. By the time he did explode into Luke's mouth, Alex had stopped being able to think of anything other than that white-hot moment of orgasm.

Gasping out a guttural growl, he came. His knees buckled. His fingers twisted through the too-short brush of Luke's hair. By the time he was able to open his eyes and draw in a breath, he was steadier on his feet. He looked down at the other man, who was staring up at him with a heavy lidded look of satisfaction.

"Holy shit," Alex said.

Luke got to his feet, seeming a little startled when Alex moved to kiss him. When Alex urged his mouth to open, Luke moaned a little. The taste of himself on Luke's tongue sent a latent thrill through Alex, still pulsing with the aftershocks of his climax.

"I wanted that," Luke said.

Alex stepped back with a nod and tucked himself into his jeans again. "Good."

"I wanted…you," Luke added.

"I don't blame you," Alex told him with a grin.

Luke smiled after a second and ducked his head, kind of shy, although when he looked up again, his gaze never wavered from Alex's. "It was good, wasn't it?"

"Fuck, yes. It was very good." Acting on an impulse he wasn't sure he understood, Alex put his hand on Luke's cheek. Then the other hand, to cup Luke's face. He brought the other man closer to him for another kiss. "You were great."

Luke hugged him and buried his face against the side of Alex's neck. Alex, unsure of what to do, put his arms around him. He patted Luke's back, hoping to hell the guy wasn't crying. When Luke stepped away, his gaze was bright, but there were no tears.

"So…do you want to go to that museum?"

Chapter 6

The Mütter Museum turned out to be a hella good time. Odd exhibits in a cool old building. Luke had been there only once before, so he was as interested in seeing everything as Alex was. They spent a couple hours viewing the exhibits, and although there was still no hand-holding or anything like that, thank God, Alex found himself looking at Luke often. Thinking about that blowjob. Thinking about kissing him.

They had dinner in a tiny Korean restaurant Alex found by searching his phone. They shared an appetizer and bites of their main dishes off the chopsticks Luke handled with impressive aplomb.

"I'm not a total redneck hick," Luke told him when Alex must've seemed surprised. He waved the chopsticks in the air. "I like country bars. That doesn't make me ridiculous."

Alex had the sense to be chagrined, an uncommon reaction for him. "Point taken."

"So…what brought you to Philly?" Luke delicately plucked a couple of shrimp from the dish in front of him to tuck into his mouth, leaving his lips glistening sensually with grease in a way Alex knew he didn't realize. "Business?"

"Yeah. Sort of. Mostly the airport." Alex laughed at Luke's face. "A buddy of mine that I met in Japan promised to help me with some leads on jobs here, and he's in Harrisburg. The Philadelphia airport was the most convenient flight for when I was coming from Europe. I ended up here, and since I'm between jobs right now, figured it was as good a place as any to crash for a while."

"What do you do?"

Alex took a few bites of his noodles and washed them down with a slug of beer before answering. "Mostly cause trouble."

"Uh huh." Luke laughed and shrugged. "I work at the Wawa. I'm trying to get a teaching job. Math. Middle school. It's harder than I thought it was going to be."

"Wow. Middle school math."

Luke nodded. "Yeah. I'm starting to think I'm going to have to apply somewhere else. Move away."

"Would that be bad?" Alex tilted his head to study the other man.

"I think people would miss me." Luke said this without so much as a hint of arrogance.

Alex's mouth twisted momentarily. "I couldn't wait to get the hell out of my town. I went as far away as I could."

"Have you ever been back?"

"Yes." Alex thought about saying more, but did not.

"And?"

Alex shook his head. "And nothing. It was the same hellhole it had always been. I never want to go back there, if I can help it."

His phone began to jangle from his pocket, the distinctive guitar line of AC/DC's *Back in Black*. Jamie. Alex pulled the phone from his pocket and slid a finger along the screen to send the call to voicemail. He looked up to see Luke staring at him curiously.

"An old friend," Alex said. "I'll call him back later."

He probably wouldn't. At least not tonight. It was only the second time James had tried calling. He didn't even know for sure that Alex was back in the States, and that was okay with Alex. He wasn't ready yet.

"Boyfriend?"

Alex shook his head. Luke nodded and concentrated on his meal. He sat back with a sigh to drink some water.

"Do you have a boyfriend?" he asked abruptly.

Alex snort-laughed. "If I did, would I be fucking you in a hotel?"

"I don't know. Would you?"

Just because that might be true didn't mean Alex had to like it. His phone buzzed. Voicemail.

"Maybe you should call him back," Luke said.

Alex frowned. "Look, it's not really any of your fucking business, okay? But he's not my boyfriend. If he *was* my boyfriend, I wouldn't be here with you."

"It's not my business, you're right."

Alex finished his bottle of beer and scowled. "You're not my boyfriend, either. Just so we're clear."

"I didn't think I was." Luke's eyebrows rose. "I don't *want* to be, either."

Something in his tone didn't sit right with Alex. He couldn't be insulted by it, since he was the one making sure Luke knew there was nothing more between them beyond a few good times. But somehow, he was.

"I'm an awesome boyfriend," Alex said after a minute.

Luke laughed. "I doubt that."

"The fuck is that supposed to mean?"

"You make eyes at everyone who walks through the

door. Or they're hitting on you. If you were someone's boyfriend, they'd never be able to relax." Luke shrugged.

"You mean they wouldn't be able to trust me?"

Luke looked him over, assessing. "I don't know you well enough to know that for sure. I just see how people look at you. How you look at them. You already told me, you're an equal opportunity slut. That would be really hard for anyone to handle."

"When I'm with someone I…." Alex could not bring himself to use the word "love." "I'm totally capable of being faithful, when I want to be."

"I guess, personally, I'd always worry about whether or not you wanted to be. Anyway, when you say it like that, you make it sound like some people don't have a choice, that cheating is something they can't help. But everyone is capable of being faithful, Alex. It's always *only* if they want to be." Luke said the last in a low, grating tone. His eyes never leaving Alex's, he downed his beer and set the bottle on the table with a thump.

"Can I get you guys anything else?" The hot little server who'd taken their orders was back. She flicked a glance at Luke, but gave Alex her full attention. "Something else from the bar? Dessert?"

"I think we're good," Luke said.

She glanced at him again, her demeanor professional. She looked back at Alex. "You sure? I'd hate for you to go away…hungry."

"Yeah, man," Luke cut in when Alex didn't answer. His tone was both amused and annoyed. "Wouldn't want you to go away hungry."

Irritated, out of sorts for a reason he didn't want to examine, Alex turned his grin on the server. Full force. She'd probably thought she was the one doing the flirting, he thought, but she had no. Fucking. Clue.

"I do have an insatiable appetite," he said to her.

The server looked a little stunned before she rallied. "I'd be happy to help you appease it. Just let me know if there's anything else I can get you. Anything."

"Just the check," Alex said.

When she brought it back to slide in front of Alex, it had her number scrawled on it. He signed the credit card slip and tucked the receipt with her number into his pocket. Luke didn't say a word as they gathered their jackets and headed out. The restaurant was only a block or so from the river, so they could walk back along it in the direction of his hotel, and that's what Alex started doing without so much as a comment. Luke followed.

Alex's phone rang again. *Back in Black*. Jamie. Again, he didn't answer. Again the phone chimed with a voicemail. He hadn't yet listened to the first one.

"He really wants to talk to you," Luke said.

Alex whirled on him. "What difference does it make to you?"

"I know, none of my business. Shit, dude. I'm sorry, okay? I don't know how to fucking navigate this. I'm sorry I hurt your feelings. I was just being honest." Luke's voice rose as he kept the pace with Alex. "Let me just grab a ride from here. You can go call that waitress, take her home. She was obviously angling for it."

"Maybe I will," Alex said.

Luke waved an angry hand. "Fine by me, what the hell do I care?"

"What *do* you care?" Alex stopped walking.

Luke kept going for a step or two before stopping himself. He turned back. "I don't!"

"Fine," Alex snapped. He tore the receipt out of his pocket and held it up. "Maybe I will call her. Maybe I'll invite her over to my room. Maybe I'll go down on her, eat that sweet pussy until she screams, then fuck her until she can't walk."

"Go ahead!"

Alex tore the paper into pieces and shoved it into the open trash can nearest him. It reeked of old garbage and piss. He felt instantly dirty from the stink of it. Cities stank. He should get out of here. Find someplace clean and quiet. A small town.

"Fuck you," he said to Luke without looking at him. "I don't even fucking know you. And I don't owe you shit."

Luke made a low noise, but didn't come any closer. Alex pulled out his phone to use the maps function to get his bearings. His hotel was easily walkable from here, if he wanted to try and figure it out and who knew, risk getting jumped along the way.

"I'm sorry," Luke said.

Alex held up his phone. He was breathing too hard and hated himself for letting this guy get that level of a reaction out of him. "Who calls me and what they want from me is none of your goddamned business. Who I take home and fuck, also none of your business."

"I know. I know. I'm sorry," Luke repeated, then again, softer.

The two beers Alex had during dinner had given him a warmth close to a buzz, but he was far from drunk. He had no excuses for his tone or his words. He was an asshole, simply that. "You're nobody to me."

Luke didn't argue the point. He took two steps back. In the flash of light from the streetlamp, his mouth had gone thin and pinched. His fists clenched at his sides.

"I picked you up in a fucking country bar," Alex continued.

In his hand, his phone rang again. Jamie, again. He

wanted to turn and throw the phone into the river as hard as he could. Watch it sink, still ringing.

He didn't realize he'd walked to the edge of the concrete wall overlooking the water, phone raised, until Luke appeared beside him. He grabbed Alex's wrist, but gently, and lowered it. With his other hand, he took the phone from Alex and tucked it into Alex's front jeans pocket.

They stood close enough for Alex to smell the beer on Luke's breath and the undertone of his cologne. Something frat boys would wear, Alex thought, shaking with anger. Shaking with something, anyway.

When Luke put his arms around him, Alex didn't fight the embrace. He pushed his face against the side of Luke's neck to breathe in the warm, male scent of him. He closed his eyes. Not crying, nothing as stupid as that.

"You don't even know me," Alex said.

Luke's hand came up to thread through Alex's hair, resting on the back of his neck. "That's okay."

"I'm not asking you to come home with me tonight," Alex said.

Luke just squeezed the back of Alex's neck and stepped back with a smile. "That's okay, too."

Chapter 7

The leads Alex had on the freelance consulting stuff had panned out in a big way. He wanted to think it had everything to do with his resumé and not the tight pants he'd worn to the meeting or the flirting he'd done with the head of HR, who he knew for a fact was unhappily fucking the guy who'd interviewed him. He knew that because Patrick, the lawyer he'd met in Japan before everything had gone to shit, had kept him up on the gossip chain. In the end, did it matter? Not when it got Alex some work. He would owe Patrick, though, and he didn't like owing anyone anything.

He hadn't spoken to Luke since the Tuesday they'd spent at the Mütter Museum and the argument they'd had after. They'd shared a cab, dropping Alex at his hotel and taking Luke on home to wherever he lived. They hadn't kissed goodbye, but that might have been because Alex was still being pissy or because Luke didn't want the cab driver to see him kissing a dude. It was hard to say, and Alex was irritated with himself for even thinking about the reasons why.

The messages from Jamie had started off lighthearted but gotten darker. He'd been drinking. Alec could hear it in the growing slur of his words and the pleading tone in his best friend's voice.

"You don't have to come home," Jamie's last message had said. "Just tell me where you are. I'll come there."

Alex had not yet returned his friend's call. He wasn't sure what he could possibly say. He couldn't talk to Jamie the way they'd always done in the past. That had been in what Alex would now always think of as *before*.

Before Anne.

Now he was in the *after*, and only time was going to make any of it better. Maybe not even that. Every day he woke up thinking he might stop thinking about her, might stop aching, that she would slip from his mind as easily as the turning of a page in a book he wanted to finish.

Anne was not a page in a book. She was the entire fucking novel, a story without a happy ending, and not even Alex was dumb enough to reach out to her husband and try to pretend that none of it had happened.

Jamie never mentioned Anne in the phone calls. That was unexpected. Jamie typically was a rug sweeper. That he was saying nothing meant he knew exactly how much had happened and what it all had meant. He never even spoke her name, not even in passing. Jamie knew it all.

Alex had checked out of the hotel to spend a few days traveling to Pittsburgh for some consulting work, then to follow up on the offer for a multi-month gig not so far from Philly in good old Chocolatetown, USA. Hershey. The money was nice, and the work would keep him busy. Hershey was a small town in the center of Pennsylvania, a couple hours from Philadelphia, a couple from Baltimore, DC, just a few longer to New York City. Even if he only spent a short time there, it would be enough, he thought.

Enough to get him back on his feet. Enough to get him on track. To settle him. So far, though, he hadn't taken it. He did, however, go back to Philadelphia.

"Welcome back, Mr. Kennedy." The front desk clerk's broad grin held no hint of flirtation, something Alex appreciated. "Your luggage was taken up to your room. You're on the sixth floor this time."

"Great. Thanks." Alex took the fresh keys and made his way to the sixth floor.

The new room was identical to the old room, except reversed. He laughed at that, thinking that if he were to get stoned or shithammered drunk that he would end up pissing in the trash can at the side of the bed instead of the toilet. Getting stoned or shithammered suddenly sounded like the best idea he'd had in the past week.

Do a little drinking. A little smoking. Maybe some pills. Get drunk, get high, get laid. A perfect Friday night, one guaranteed to erase any guilt he felt about not answering Jamie's messages.

In the shower, Alex bent his head beneath the hot spray of water and closed his eyes. He'd taken a couple shots from his almost empty bottle of Jameson before coming in, and his head was pleasantly buzzing. His hands moved over his body, assessing it. A little thicker here, in the places he pinched. Muscled unexpectedly here, from walking so much all around the city. His face, scruffy with the bristle of beard he'd been letting grow in, although he almost always preferred to be clean-shaven. His hair, too, had grown overlong, but he felt no urge to cut it.

Beneath the water, he got on his hands and knees. Eyes closed. He wanted to cry, but couldn't find the tears. He didn't deserve them, he thought. He didn't deserve the release of weeping. He opened his mouth to let out a scream, but nothing came out except a hiss of air.

He was never going to see her again.

He had walked away from her because it was the right thing to do. He had broken her; he had slaughtered himself. It was the right thing to do. The right and best thing. The most awful thing.

He loved her, and he would never be with her, and he had chosen that when there had been the chance for something else. A moment in time when if only he'd had the courage to be happy, everything might have changed.

Everything changes, Alex thought.

If he could turn back the time, if she could forgive him, he thought, then maybe he could learn to…what? What could he learn? To feel? To trust? To fucking *love*, the way other people did? He would never be good for anyone but himself, and he couldn't even be counted on to be that.

The whiskey had hit him harder than he'd thought it would. An empty stomach. Melancholy. Emotions surged over him, and he gave up to it a little because of the hot shower and his sudden and utterly brutal loneliness.

He loved her, Anne Kinney. His best friend Jamie's wife. Jamie had invited him into their marriage, but Alex had been the one to take advantage. To step too far. He'd been selfish and greedy in his love. It had never been meant to become so much, but oh, God, it had, and now he tried so hard to weep and found nothing but an empty and barren desert where his tears ought to have been.

Alex got to his feet. He tipped his head back to let the hot water fill his mouth. To wash over his eyes, still closed. His hands moved over his body. Between his legs, to his soft cock. It took a few strokes to get it to respond.

He deliberately did not think of Anne.

He could not let himself imagine her. The flavor of her kisses. The scent of her. The sounds she made when she came. He could not let himself remember how it had felt when she put her arms around him, how the rest of the world had faded away and become something he thought he might be able to bear, if only he could face it along with her.

Now, he thought of Luke. That hard body. The bristle brush cut of blond hair. His smile, sometimes shy or innocent or self-effacing. The sound of his voice when he came.

In his fist, Alex's cock rose. Thick and hard and eager to seek pleasure. He groaned into the spray of water, thinking about how it had felt to slide into Luke's tight but welcoming asshole. How the other man's body had gripped him. How Luke had moaned and moved so eagerly.

He thought, too, of the suction of Luke's lips and tongue on his cock. How good it had been to give up to those sensations. That pleasure. How it had wiped away everything but desire.

Alex muttered out a groan and came in thick spurts, opening his eyes to watch as the white come jetted out into the shower spray and was washed away into the drain. His cock pulsed and throbbed in his fist. His thighs strained with the effort. The hand he'd put up on the shower wall curled into a fist.

He closed his eyes again, breathing hard and grateful for the hotel shower's unlimited hot water. The orgasm hadn't drained him. It had put him in a better mood, for sure. It had given him some energy.

Alex was ready…for something.

He pulled on a pair of slim fitting jeans. No briefs. A dark blue v-necked t-shirt, also fitted. Fingers dragging through his hair, he left it tousled and kept the faint shadow of his beard. He didn't bother looking at his reflection. He knew too well what his face looked like, and since it almost never let him down, he wasn't going to worry about it now.

He'd rarely had a problem going out dancing and drinking on his own. He might start out the evening alone, but he never ended up that way…unless he wanted to. Dressed and ready to go with a slow sipping of the last of his Jameson warming his belly, Alex mapped the best way to get to the club. A cab looked like the best bet, so he called for one. He'd have enough time to finish his drink.

He had time to make a phone call.

But when his fingers hovered over the screen to pull up Jamie's number, he still couldn't bring himself to do it. The buzz and hum of the liquor in his blood wasn't strong enough for him to have lost control, not quite enough to make him stupid.

He texted Luke, instead. The address of the club. A sleekly styled selfie, specifically out of focus but sexy as fuck. A command, not a request.

Meet me.

Chapter 8

Luke had not answered the text by the time Alex got to the club. That didn't matter, Alex told himself. If Luke didn't show, someone else would. Hell, maybe more than one.

He found a spot at the bar and ordered a whiskey on the rocks, but changed his mind. "No. Wait. I want something fancy."

"Bushmill's? We have twenty-five year, the Millennium. That's pretty fucking fancy," the bartender said. "Especially for this place."

"No, I mean one of those drinks with a fancy name and a lot of ingredients. Bonus if you have to put it in a specialty glass."

And that, friends, was how Alex Kennedy ended up drinking something called The Rimmer, which came in a plastic cup shaped like a pair of butt cheeks, the anus of which allowed the use of the colored bendy straw. It met all the criteria he'd demanded. It also tasted like...well, he thought as he drank with a grimace, like shit.

From his vantage point at the bar's corner, he could see

both the decent-sized dance floor and also the front doors. Every time a blond head appeared he, tensed. This was stupid. He was being an asshole. He didn't even want to see Luke again. Why would he?

Alex drained his drink and tossed the plastic cup into the can at the side of the bar. He wasn't going to be ordering another one of those, that was for sure. He pulled his phone from his front pocket, ignoring the pair of guys who'd been trying to get his attention for the past fifteen minutes by gyrating in front of him.

On my way

Relief. That was the weird feeling trickling through him. First relief, then elation. Alex shoved his phone back into his pocket and moved toward the front of the club. He had to jiggity jog around a few hightop tables, but then, there he was.

Luke was looking intense, but his face lit up at the sight of Alex. They hugged, hard but brief. Luke clapped Alex on the back. No kiss.

"You made it," Alex said.

Luke nodded, looking around. "This is a gay bar."

"Newsflash," Alex said. "We're both at least sort of gay."

"Yeah." Luke laughed, looking fucking adorable and shy, and if the club hadn't been so dark, there'd have been a blush clear on his cheeks.

"Dance with me."

Luke grinned. "Line dance?"

"I don't think they do that here," Alex said, "but maybe we'll set a trend."

It had been forever since Alex had been dancing like this, or at least that's how it felt. Light, free, unburdened — it had been much longer since he'd even drifted close to those feelings, but here he was in the center of a crush of hot guys in various stages of inebriation, all of them dancing and flirting and kissing and groping, and Alex pulled Luke close to him so they could dance together.

"You look hot tonight," Luke shouted over the pulsing bass beat.

Alex grinned and put his hands own Luke's hips to bring him in closer. "I didn't think you'd notice."

"Everyone notices."

Alex moved in close. "I don't care about everyone else."

They kissed, bruisingly hard. Luke put a hand on the back of Alex's neck, holding him close. His other one went to the small of Alex's back. They danced and kissed and ground their bodies together the way everyone was doing on the dance floor.

A tall black man, shirtless, glitter in his shorn-to-the-scalp hair, danced up behind Luke and began bumping his ass. He made eye contact with Alex in that dance club etiquette of making sure it was cool if you were going to grind up on someone else's partner. Alex watched Luke's face turn from giddy joy to concern as he half-turned to see who exactly was grinding him from behind.

"Just dance," Alex said. He fisted his hands in the front of Luke's shirt, keeping him facing forward. He watched Luke's gaze go a little hazy with arousal. "Dance, man."

They danced.

They all danced, the entire room, bumping, grinding, swaying, jumping. Hands in the air. Raising the roof. The DJ played every single dance floor anthem that had been popular in the past ten years.

Sweating, light-headed and head pounding, Alex kissed Luke again. The crowd turned them. Luke was kissing the guy who'd been dancing behind him. Alex watched them, both so beautiful, and waited to feel…jealous? He couldn't be. Everything here tonight was love, love, love…no, it was lust, lust, lust, and he was fine with that. Love was something he never wanted to feel again. Love was a thing that broke you, and he was done with breaking.

"Alex? You okay?" Luke had turned back to him, his expression still dazed.

He wasn't okay. Alex wasn't sure he was ever going to be okay again. Now was not the time; here was not the place. In the here and now, he was going to dance and kiss and grind and grope and drink, and if there was someone here who'd hook him up with something to snort or swallow, he'd do that, too.

Alex put his hands on Luke's shoulders and turned him around to face the guy who'd been kissing him. He pushed them together. A beneficent prince, urging his subjects to take care of themselves.

The night wore on and became a blur. Sweating, Alex found a spot by the wall where he could lean. His phone made its way into his hand. He wasn't going to try and make a call, but he pulled up his text window. The last text had not been from Luke, but from Jamie.

Please talk to me

Almost two in the morning. Last call had been announced. It was time to find someone to take him home. Alex's thumbs moved over the screen. He didn't know what to say except, *I'm sorry*.

Immediately, three small bouncing dots on the screen showed that Jamie was replying, but Alex swiped away the message screen and pushed his phone into his pocket. It buzzed against his thigh. He ignored it.

Luke found him. He was sweaty, his shirt opened nearly to his navel. He was grinning wildly, but looked tired, the way Alex felt.

"Let's get out of here," Alex said.

Chapter 9

"Shhh. You have to be quiet. Don't wake up the neighbors, they're nosy." Luke hiss-whispered this, but his voice trailed off into laughter as he fumbled with the lock on the basement door.

Alex was not sober, but most of the night's indulgence had started to wear off. All the dancing and sweating. He hadn't so much as glanced at his phone since he and Luke had left the club. He didn't want to see an accusatory messages waiting for him, ones he would find himself unable to answer, or worse, compelled to reply to.

"Shhh," Luke repeated. The door swung open into the darkness. He gestured. "C'mon."

Alex followed. Luke hit the wall switch, revealing an apartment of sorts with dated décor. Brown plaid furniture with wooden arms, matching wood paneling, a bar at one end with leather stools that definitely had been new probably before Luke had even been born. A small kitchenette featured a fridge, stove and sink, and through two open doors Alex glimpsed a bedroom and a bathroom.

"My place," Luke said.

Alex nodded. "Nice."

"You want some water?"

"Yeah, thanks." Alex followed Luke to the kitchen area and took the bottle of water.

He watched Luke as they both guzzled. The other guy could drink, that was for sure, but Alex wasn't surprised. He was a frat boy, barely out of college. Of course he could handle his booze.

They both drank the water in silence. It had been Luke's idea to come back here. His parents, he'd said, were away visiting an older sister who'd had a baby a few months ago. They wouldn't be back for a week. Luke could make Alex breakfast, a home-cooked meal. Something better than takeout from a coffee shop. And Alex had fallen for all of it, knowing this was probably a mistake but doing it anyway because it had been so damned long since anyone had offered to take care of him.

Luke tipped his back to get the bottle's last drops and tossed the empty bottle into the sink. He gave Alex an expectant look. Alex had not yet finished his water, but capped the bottle and set it on the countertop.

"I want you to fuck me again," Luke said.

"Of course you do."

Luke's brow furrowed. "If you don't want to, just say so."

"I want to. Of course I want to. I asked you to meet me tonight, didn't I? I came back here with you, didn't I?" In Alex's pocket, his phone pressed against his thigh. He was only imagining that it was getting hotter, ready to singe him.

He didn't want to read the messages he knew had come in. He wanted to push all that away. He did want to fuck Luke and get lost in that pleasure. He crooked a finger, drawing Luke closer.

"Kiss," Alex ordered.

Luke gave small, huffing sigh and obliged. It was sweet, that kiss, lingering and slow but tinged with heat. Luke took Alex's hand and put it on the denim-covered bulge of his crotch.

"Nobody's ever got me this hard," Luke whispered.

Alex squeezed gently, earning another moan from Luke. "What about all those fine young lads you were swapping spit with tonight?"

"Nope."

"Lucky me," Alex said. "Bedroom? Or here on the floor."

Luke shuddered. "Oh. God."

"You've thought about that, huh? The way you thought about everything else. Getting fucked right here, out in the open, right in the middle of your living room. Feels dirty, right?" Alex laughed as his hand stroked harder, and Luke once more got that hazy, dazed look in his eyes. "You want me to put you on your hands and knees and take your ass right here, don't you?"

"Yes. God, yes, please."

They both stripped quickly. Alex stroked his cock to life as he watched Luke get into exactly the position he'd been describing. Women were softer. Easier to get inside. Their bodies angled differently. But from behind, once he was in deep, sometimes it was easy to forget if he was fucking a man or a woman. The same smooth slope of a back, tautly muscled asscheeks. Gasps and moans. The clutch of flesh on his cock. It all felt good.

"Condoms?" Alex asked.

Luke straightened onto his knees, looking over his shoulder. "In the bedroom."

"Wait here. Don't move," Alex said. Commanded, really. Luke seemed to kind of like that, being bossed around. Alex could do that. Not his long-term thing, but sure, he could be dommy, sometimes.

In the bedroom, he found Luke's condom stash right where it was expected, in the nightstand. Alex took a minute or two to look around the room, being nosy. Luke was messy, clothes flung all over the place. Posters of bathing suit models all over the walls, along with a few sports heroes Alex recognized but not by name. It was a typical frat boy room, and it made Alex grin.

In the living room, Luke had stayed in place. Face down, ass up. He had great cheeks, and he'd spread his thighs so there was more than a hint of ballsack showing, along with the shadowy pucker of his asshole. He twisted when Alex came into the room.

"Your phone's been ringing," he said over his shoulder.

Alex looked automatically to his jeans, slung over the arm of an ancient orange recliner. He'd thought he'd turned the ringer off, but maybe in the struggle to get out of his jeans he'd accidentally flipped it back on. Even as he moved toward Luke and the promise of sexual oblivion, he could hear the phone ringing again.

Back in Black.

The ringtone cut off as the call went to voicemail. He got onto his knees, condom in his fist, behind Luke. He spit into his hand, ready to use that since he'd found the rubbers but no lube.

The phone rang again. Same ringtone. Jamie was calling him again. It went to voicemail.

Alex put his hands on Luke's hips. His cock had been semi-hard when he went into the bedroom, but it was softening now. He stroked it with one hand while he used the other to tease at Luke's opening. The condom was still in its package, next to him on the floor.

The phone rang again. Cut off. Rang at once. Now

Jamie wasn't leaving voicemails, he was immediately hanging up and ringing again.

Luke pushed up onto his hands and rocked back on his heels. He looked over his shoulder. "Aren't you going to answer that?"

"No."

"At least turn the ringer off?"

Alex got to his feet and went to the chair, digging into his jeans pocket for the phone. Flipping the ringer off, he slammed the phone onto the chair and turned to face Luke. The other guy got to his feet, his face first alarmed, then smoothing into an expression Alex hated.

Sympathy.

"Don't," Alex warned. "Don't say a fucking word. Either get down on the floor again and let me fuck you, just like you said you wanted, or I'm out of here."

Luke spread his fingers open with a shrug, saying nothing. He glanced toward the door to the outside. His cock was still hard. He didn't get onto his hands and knees again.

The phone, which had fallen face up on the chair, lit up and buzzed. Alex cursed and grabbed it, fumbling to get to the phone's settings screen so he could turn off even that shitty hum.

The phone rang again as he was swiping. The call connected. He heard Jamie's voice, at first hesitant and surprised. Then loud. Cursing. Pleading. Jamie sounded drunker than Alex felt right now.

Luke gently took the phone from Alex's shaking hands. "Hello? Hey. Alex can't take your call right now, okay?"

Alex couldn't hear what happened after that because he was stumbling to the bathroom, sure he was going to lose every single drink he'd had the entire night. He managed to keep it all in his stomach, although he hovered over the toilet with his mouth open and several nasty tasting strands of drool dangling before he was finally able to swallow them. He sat on the edge of the tub and put his face in his hands.

Luke knocked gently on the door, which was open, but stood in the doorway at a respectful distance. "You okay? You need anything?"

"No. I'm going to go home. To the hotel. It's not home. I call it that, but it's not. I don't have a home anymore."

"You don't have to do that," Luke said. "In fact, I don't think you should. It's fucking late, man. And you're not in any shape to be trying to get yourself anywhere but into bed. Just stay here. It'll all be fine. Okay?"

After a moment, Alex nodded. Luke took him to the bedroom. Gave him another bottle of water and stood over him while he drank it, garbage pail at hand in case Alex needed it. He didn't. He wasn't sick because of the drinks, although he couldn't tell Luke that. He was sick because of Jamie.

Luke turned off the lights. Turned on a floor fan to provide white noise and a sweeping band of irregular coolness that was surprisingly refreshing, considering the entire basement flat was nothing close to being warm. He plumped the pillows and drew a sheet over Alex up to his waist, but he didn't try to cuddle.

"I told him you'd call him back tomorrow, when you were awake," Luke said into the darkness. "He said to tell you that he was sorry about everything, and that he wasn't mad or anything, he just wanted you to call him. He said for you to please, please just call him."

Alex said nothing.

Luke turned onto his side to face him. "He sounded pretty bad off, Alex."

Alex closed his eyes and opened them again. There was

so little difference between the backs of his eyelids and the basement bedroom that he almost couldn't be sure if he had his eyes open or not. He closed them again, wishing for sleep.

"Do you love him?" Luke asked quietly.

"He's my best friend."

Luke huffed a sigh. "So. Yes."

"It's not like that," Alex replied, weary and torn down.

"Could it be like that? If you let it?"

Alex couldn't find an answer to that. The bed dipped and shifted as Luke rolled onto his side. He nudged Alex hard enough to turn him over, so Luke could spoon him. His big hand went flat over Alex's heart. His breath was hot on the back of Alex's neck.

"Go to sleep, dude," Luke murmured. "Things always look better in the morning."

Chapter 10

The shrieking woke Alex from a sound sleep so deep he hadn't even been dreaming. He bolted upright, feet hitting the floor and his fists up before he could even make sense of what was happening. The entire room whirled around him as he blinked, trying to focus in the dark basement room.

It took him a good thirty seconds to figure out where the hell he was. Through the open bedroom door he could see the rest of Luke's apartment. Voices, one low and soothing, the other high-pitched and hysterical, came from just out of sight. Alex considered going to the doorway to see what was happening, but common sense, a thing with which he was not usually connected, convinced him to hang back and eavesdrop. He had to piss something fierce, though. He couldn't stay in the bedroom forever. He started looking for something to pee into, though, just in case.

"You said it wasn't me! That's what you told me, it wasn't me!" The feminine voice screeched this, then dissolved into loud, braying sobs.

Luke's voice, a placating mutter, words indistinct, came next. Alex couldn't make out exactly what he was saying, but he had a good guess. Whoever the girl was out in the living room, he imagined she'd gotten an eyeful of something she wasn't expecting. The fact that Luke had never mentioned a girlfriend was irritating, not that Alex had the right to be annoyed. He hadn't pictured Luke as a cheater, but as the owner of a glass house, Alex wasn't about to toss so much as a pebble.

"You're fucking disgusting!" The girl screamed again.

The crack of flesh on flesh had Alex moving toward the door. If Luke was resorting to physical violence, someone needed to stop him. As it turned out, Luke wasn't the one doing the smacking.

The small blonde had her hair done in a high ponytail. She wore skinny jeans and cowboy boots. Lots of cleavage. A belly button ring glinted from beneath the hem of her tank top. At the sight of Alex she let out a long, guttering cry and hammered Luke across the face again.

The guy took it without a word, but when she tried to hit him a third time, Alex stepped up. "Stop that."

"You don't tell me what to do! Disgusting faggot!" The words choked out of her. She actually turned her face to spit to the side.

"Classy," Alex said with a glance at Luke, who looked miserable but wasn't saying anything.

The girl yanked at a ring on her, oh shit, left hand. She waved it around. "And you can take your goddamned ring back!"

"I told you I didn't want it back," Luke said. "You keep it."

"I don't want anything you ever gave me." She'd stopped screaming, at least. She looked at Alex, her gaze scanning his naked body. Her lip curled, and then she looked simply defeated. "Jesus, I hope you didn't actually give me something."

Luke took a step toward her, then. He, at least, wore a pair of briefs. He put out a hand, but she jerked away from it.

"I'm sorry," he said.

"Fuck you," the girl told him. She slammed the ring onto the half-bar separating the kitchen area from the living room. "You and your boyfriend can eat shit."

"He's not…" Luke began, but she flipped him off and went out the door, slamming it behind her.

In the silence that followed, Alex's urge to pee rose to unignorable levels. By the time he got out of the bathroom, Luke had seated himself at the bar. Head in his hands. The ring glittered on the counter next to him.

Alex took the barstool next to him and put a hand on his shoulder. "Always make sure you get the key back, dude."

"She used the one under the rock. She wanted to surprise me."

Alex laughed. "Someone got surprised, all right."

"It's not funny," Luke said.

Alex's chuckle faded. He squeezed Luke's shoulder. "You're right, it's not. I'm sorry."

"I do love her." Luke swiped at his face. "I wanted to marry her. I think I still might want to. I don't know. Maybe she'll forgive me."

Alex let go of the other man and got up from the stool to make his way around the bar. He found the coffeemaker and the filters next to it. Filled the carafe. Added the coffee from the package next to the filters. He spoke as he made the coffee, not looking at Luke.

"She might forgive you. She might not even make you pay for it for the rest of your life, but that doesn't seem likely. Someone who calls someone else a disgusting faggot isn't going to forget that she found you in bed with a naked guy." He turned, then, as the coffeemaker burbled happily behind him. "I'm sure you do love her, man, but you should give a long, hard think about spending your life with the kind of person who hates like that."

Luke shook his head. "She's not like that."

"Obviously, she is," Alex pointed out with a shrug.

"She was surprised. She was…" Luke's voice softened and trailed off.

Alex shrugged again. "When someone shows you who they really are, man, you should always pay attention."

Luke nodded. His eyes were red-rimmed. His mouth twisted into a miserable frown. He put his face in his hands again, and his shoulders lifted and fell with a heavy, grieving sigh.

Alex filled a mug with coffee and pushed it in front of the other guy. He filled one for himself and sipped it. Silent. He wasn't sure what else he could say.

"I shouldn't have brought you here," Luke said in a low voice.

"Probably not," Alex agreed. "But you did."

Luke looked up. He drank some coffee. Put the mug down. Nodded.

"She's going to tell everyone I'm a fag. Queer," Luke corrected. "Gay. Shit. What am I supposed to call it?"

"You don't have to call 'it' anything. You're attracted to men and women. You don't owe anyone an explanation about that. It's not anyone's business where you put your dick unless you're fucking them with it," Alex said, a little harder than he'd intended to. He softened his voice. "Look, I'm the last motherfucker to be giving out relationship advice, okay? I've never had one that lasted or worked. I've been a complete asshole to just about everyone who's ever given me the time of day."

"You haven't been an asshole to me."

Alex laughed. "Give it time."

Luke groaned and stretched, then drank more coffee. He set the mug on the counter next to the ring. He picked it up and held it to the light. "What do I do with this?"

"Sell it. Go on a trip around the world."

"It might buy me a trip to the Wawa," Luke said.

Alex put a hand over his mouth to make a dainty "ooh!" They both laughed. Luke looked better than he had a few minutes ago.

From the coffee table, Alex's phone rang.

"Are you going to answer it?" Luke asked.

Alex shook his head. Luke frowned. They both drank their coffee in silence as the phone went quiet, too. After a few seconds, the voicemail tone beeped.

"You can't avoid him forever, man. And I don't think you want to, anyway."

Alex clenched his jaw. "It's a fucked up situation, that's all. I made a huge mess of things, and I don't know how to fix them."

"Maybe he doesn't need you to fix them. Maybe he just wants to…you know. Move on."

A short bark of a laugh burst from Alex's throat, painful and tearing. "It's not just about him. Fuck. It's barely about him."

"So…who's it about?"

Alex had finished his coffee, and his stomach protested at the thought of drinking any more. He tried to make a joke. Play it all off. He tried to get mad, insulted, that Luke thought he could try to get in Alex's business. All he could manage was a small, sad sigh.

"Her name," he said, "is Anne."

Chapter 11

"I didn't go to their wedding," Alex said. Luke had made good on his promise of making breakfast, and although he'd thought he wouldn't be able to stand a bite of it, Alex's stomach was rumbling at the smell of frying bacon and eggs. He'd already devoured a piece of toast laid thick with butter and jam. "He invited me, of course, but I was an asshole and didn't go. I couldn't watch him walking down the aisle, I guess because I was jealous that he'd found someone and I hadn't, maybe? I mean, not something that was going to last."

Luke slid a plate in front of him and took one for himself. "You weren't jealous because he was marrying someone who wasn't you?"

"No. Jesus, no." Alex gave a genuine laugh. "I told you. It's not like that. And no, it can't ever be like that."

"But he wants you like that," Luke offered.

Alex was quiet for a minute while he chewed and swallowed, thinking how to answer. When his mouth was clear, he said, "I think Jamie wants, yeah. The way you've been wanting. I think he won't admit it, and he tells himself that it's me. Just me."

"You sure it's not just you?" Luke shoveled a forkful of dripping eggs onto his toast and bit into it.

Again, Alex thought. "I don't know. I don't want it to be just me."

"Because he's married?"

"Because if I lose Jamie as my friend, I have nothing left." The words clipped out of him before he could stifle them. Alex focused on his plate, not looking at Luke.

"He's called you like, a million times. This isn't a guy who's going away, Alex."

Alex hunched his shoulders before forcing himself to sit up straight. He dragged his fork through the eggs and bacon on his plate, stabbing another bite but not taking it. He shook his head.

"So. What about her? Anne."

"I thought it would be fun. Jamie said she wanted to be with two guys. It wasn't the first time I'd ever been into something a little off-center that way. If anything, it felt like a great way to spend the summer. Getting laid. You know? That was all it was supposed to be."

"But it wasn't?"

Alex shook his head. "I wasn't supposed to fall in love with her. She belongs to Jamie."

"You think anyone can ever really belong to someone else? That surprises me. I didn't figure you for the possessive sort." Luke ate another bite of sloppy breakfast, chewing with a small sound of appreciation that turned Alex toward him.

Alex was, as he'd told Luke, totally capable of being faithful when he wanted to be. He'd also been the other man more than once, so it was obvious he didn't have some medieval idea about romantic ownership, not that Luke would know any of that. "It was different with them."

"Because you love him. And you fell in love with her. The three of you couldn't just work it out?"

"No!" Alex recoiled.

Luke didn't look offended at the vehemence of his answer. "Why?"

"Because…" Alex coughed into his fist, reluctant to put any of this into words. He'd spent so long trying not to think about it at all. He pictured his feelings as being buried under mounds of garbage, Luke handing him a shovel. He was going to have to dig, and hard, to get to the bottom. It was going to smell horrible. It might make him sick. No. It would *definitely* make him sick.

"You love her?"

"Yes. Shit. Yes. I do, I love her," Alex answered in a strained voice. "But I'm no good for anyone else."

"Why do you keep saying that?" Luke put a hand on Alex's shoulder, turning him on the bar stool so they faced each other.

Alex looked into Luke's eyes. "Because it's the truth."

"You know one of the first things you said to me was that you weren't ashamed of who you are. That you weren't going to be the rationale for my self-hatred. But you hate yourself a lot, man. I don't know why, but you do." They'd both slid into sweatpants for breakfast but remained shirtless. Luke's fingers squeezed gently before sliding down Alex's bare arm.

Alex's skin goosepimpled under the touch. He had no answer, but then Luke had made a statement, not asked a question.

"I don't want to lose him."

"You were okay with losing her? Even though you love her?"

"It wouldn't have worked out for me and her, not in the long term. Not the way it started. I couldn't hurt Jamie that way. I gave her up, so I wouldn't have to lose him."

Luke nodded slowly. "But you're going to, Alex, unless you can at least face him."

When Alex didn't answer him, Luke leaned to kiss him on the mouth. He tasted of butter and jam, bacon and coffee. The kiss was brief, but sweet. When Luke moved to pull back, Alex grabbed his bicep and held it. They kissed again, harder this time.

Still kissing, the two of them got off the barstools and managed to get to the bedroom. With both wearing only Luke's sweatpants, it was easy to get naked. Luke took Alex's stiffening cock in his hand, still kissing him. The other went to the small of Alex's back. Their bodies met, hard cocks pressing between them.

Luke broke the kiss to slide his teeth along Alex's jaw, earning a moan. Then along his throat. He nipped lightly at Alex's collarbones and dipped lower to sample one nipple, then the other. All the while, his hand stroked, stroked, palming the head of Alex's cock. Moving down to his balls, then up the shaft again.

"Fuck," Luke said as he drew his fingertip over the swollen head of Alex's prick to capture the silver bead of fluid gathered there. He tucked it into his mouth with a smile.

The sight of that grin sent a flood of arousal through Alex, fierce enough to surprise him. Yeah, he was into Luke's body, and the fucking they'd already done had been good enough for him to want more of it. But there was more here, whether Alex was willing to admit it or not, and the sensual way Luke tasted him was part of that. It was an intimacy he hadn't felt for a while, and although Alex was a fan of the one-night stand, there was no denying that sex usually got better with familiarity and friendship.

On the bed, Luke moved between Alex's thighs. He took the thickness of Alex's dick into his mouth, sucking gently and adding a flick of his tongue along the underside of the head. Fuck, that felt good, and once again, Alex was letting himself get lost inside the wonderful glow of sexual arousal. Desire could and would push away everything else, until it was all he had to think about and nothing else.

He ran his hand over Luke's head, seeking to dig his fingers into Luke's hair, but of course he'd forgotten that it was too short. Alex satisfied himself with twisting his fingers into the bedsheets, instead. He lifted his hips, thrusting into the savory heat of Luke's mouth. At the exploratory probe of Luke's finger against his asshole, though, Alex tensed.

"No?" Luke paused to murmur.

"It's fine. Just wasn't expecting it."

"I've never done it," Luke said after a second. "I'll do my best."

Alex pushed onto his elbows to look down at the other man. "Lube. Lots of lube. And take your time."

"Got it." Luke laughed and grabbed a bottle of lube from under the bed. That explained why Alex hadn't found it when he was looking for the condoms.

Alex lay back, closing his eyes. He was usually the one in charge, even if he was the one being done to instead of doing. He relaxed again into the pleasure.

Luke's slick finger pushed inside him, slowly. It wasn't hitting him exactly right, not at first, but the mouth action on his cock was working just fine. Then Luke shifted his hand a little and yes, oh fuck.

"There," Alex gasped hoarsely. "Yeah. Fuck. Right there. Like that."

"Like this?" Luke curled his finger, pressing firmly against that magic spot.

"Yes." Alex rocked his hips.

The pleasure rose, up and up. Luke hadn't quite mastered the blowjob or ringing the back doorbell, but he was making a valiant effort at both. It was good and getting better. When the orgasm came, it was fast. Hard. Powerful. Alex cried out with it, a harsh, gravelled gasp that became a moan. Panting, he arched and fell back on the bed. Spent.

He'd had a shit night's sleep and an orgasm. Add that to a belly full of breakfast, and there was no real option. He was going to be the worst kind of inconsiderate lover and fall asleep without reciprocating.

As he did, Alex was only half-aware of Luke moving up beside him to pull the sheets over them both. They didn't spoon, but Luke's big hand rested on Alex's naked hip. Their feet touched.

"You wouldn't have nothing left," Luke said, and then Alex was out.

Chapter 12

Alex woke, thank God not to screaming this time, but to the smell of something good and the sound of a country music song on low volume. He didn't listen to much country, but he supposed he didn't have to be familiar with the artist or the song to know what it was about. Cheating lover, broken heart, big ol' truck. It seemed pretty standard.

Luke turned from the small stove as Alex padded from the bedroom on bare feet. He'd dressed in his own clothes. He settled himself onto a bar stool.

"I'm making burgers. Hope that's okay?"

"All we've done today is eat and fuck," Alex said. "But hell yeah. I love a good burger."

He yawned and stretched and watched Luke work at the stove. The other guy had dressed in a pair of baggy jeans, a gray t-shirt, a flannel overtop it. He flipped the burgers and slid them onto a plate, then pulled a pan of fries out of the oven and set them on a trivet to cool. He added a couple cheese slices to the meat and handed Alex a bag of rolls.

"It's not gourmet, but I was starving. I wasn't sure when you were going to wake up."

Alex didn't have his phone handy — it was still over there on the coffee table. He looked for a clock but couldn't find one. "What time is it?"

"Close to two." Luke took a seat next to him and started to load his burger with condiments. "I have to go to work in a couple hours. You can stay here if you want to."

"Nah. I'll head back to my hotel." Alex eyed the burger before biting it. It was good, and he realized he, too, was starving.

"You sure?" Luke's voice had taken on a forced casual tone. "I'll be back by eleven-thirty. That's not too late."

Alex bit, chewed, swallowed. He wiped his mouth with a paper napkin Luke had put out. "I'm not going to hang around your apartment while you're at work, man. That's a little too much, don't you think?"

"I didn't think so, or else I wouldn't have offered. I thought maybe you'd like being able to spread out a little, that's all." Luke now sounded stiff.

"Nah. I'm good." Alex kept his own tone light and casual.

Neither of them looked at each other.

When he'd finished eating, Alex took his plate and Luke's, too, to the sink. He washed the pan Luke had used to make the burgers. He could feel Luke watching him, but didn't turn.

"You don't have to do that," Luke said.

Alex shrugged. "You cooked. I'll clean up."

The barstool scraped as Luke pushed it back. He went into the bathroom. The shower came on. Alex finished doing the dishes, but left them in the drainer since he didn't know where they went, and he wasn't about to dig around in Luke's cupboards. By the time

Luke got out of the bathroom, Alex had gathered his things.

"I'm just going to get out of here," he said. He needed a shower and a toothbrush. More than that, he needed to be alone.

Luke nodded. "Fine."

It wasn't fine. Alex could tell that from the guy's expression and the way he sounded, and fuck, why did it always have to get like this? Complicated?

Alex turned. "I've known James Kinney since we were dumbfuck kids. He's the only person in my whole fucking miserable life who ever made me feel like I was worth a goddamned thing…until Anne."

Luke said nothing.

"I used to think Jamie would be the only person who could ever made me understand what it was like to love someone. Then he invited me to stay with them for the summer. He invited me to be with his wife. Not to fuck her. Everything but that." Alex let out low, coughing laugh that hurt his throat. He ran a hand through his hair, pushing it out of his eyes. The words spilled out of him, hot and bitter as bile. "But you know what, man? It wasn't about whether or not I was allowed to put my cock inside her pussy. Because we did fuck. Just the once. At the end. By then it was too late. I was leaving. I had to go. I had to leave them both, because I couldn't figure out a way that any of it could ever work. Not long term. I wasn't supposed to be real, you know? I was something Jamie wanted and couldn't have, so he offered me to her as a way to somehow, some way, maybe just…taste it. Just fucking taste it, for a little while."

A grinding sob broke free of Alex's throat. He tried to stifle it, but it was like swallowing barbed wire. Tearing. He swore he could taste blood.

"I've loved him from the first time I saw him in his fucking pink alligator shirt with the collar up. I loved him even when he punched me in the face and called me a fucking fairy faggot queer, when we went through a glass coffee table together. When I took him to the ER." Alex's fists clenched, his muscles tensing at the awful memory. He looked at Luke, whose expression had twisted in dismay. "I loved him, and then I loved her. And I hate him for that. I fucking hate that motherfucker for giving me just a little taste, for just a little while."

Luke advanced a step or two, like he meant to take Alex into his arms. Alex backed up, hands in front of him. He didn't want to be hugged or touched or stroked or soothed. He wanted to get out of this apartment, away from Luke, back to his sterile hotel room where he could be alone and force all of this away.

"I'm going to go," Alex said.

Luke nodded hesitantly, looking warily hopeful. "Will you call me? Can I call you?"

"No."

"Jesus, you're hard," Luke said.

"You barely know me," Alex told him bluntly. "We fucked. We had a good time. That's all this is or all it ever was. I'm glad to have been part of your journey or whatever the fuck you're about to say, but that's all."

Luke recoiled like Alex had punched him in the face. He didn't say anything, but what could there be to say, really? Alex put his hand on the doorknob. He waited, but only half a minute, for Luke to call after him and was relieved when all that followed him was silence.

Chapter 13

There was no epiphany. No moment of clarity. Jamie had simply worn him down. Alex had agreed to meet him in a hotel room at the Philadelphia airport, where James would be flying in for one night.

Alex hadn't asked where Anne would be.

He had considered getting drunk or stoned before heading over, but in the end had decided he didn't want to be impaired while facing Jamie. That might mean Alex was finally getting to be a grownup. It might mean he leaned a little more toward the masochistic end of the spectrum. Either way, Alex showed up to Jamie's room sober.

He knocked. The door opened at once, like Jamie had been standing behind it, waiting. They both stood there in silence for a few seconds. The look on Jamie's face — hope, desperation, a little fear, twisted Alex's heart into his throat. Jamie stepped aside to let him in and closed the door behind him.

"Hey, man." Jamie moved as though he meant to hug

Alex, but held back so obviously it was like a forcefield had brought him up short.

Once, Jamie wouldn't have hesitated to embrace him. It made Alex feel like shit, and he knew it was all his fault. He reached for Jamie. Just a hand, ready to pull it back if Jamie didn't take it. Jamie did.

Their hands clasped, grasped. Alex tugged. Jamie moved toward him. They hugged, hard, a bro hug for sure, minus the back-slapping. It softened after a few seconds. Jamie buried his face against Alex's neck.

Alex held him.

Only that, not wanting to let go, not wanting Jamie to let go, either. Dampness on his neck. Jamie's tears.

Alex clung tighter, a hand stroking over Jamie's hair, then cupping the back of his neck. He whispered, "Don't, please. Don't."

Jamie pulled away to look at him. "I'm sorry, man. I'm so fucking sorry—"

"Don't," Alex said again. "You don't have to be sorry. Okay?"

"But it's my fault everything got so fucked up," Jamie insisted. "I should never have set it all up. I should never have asked you to fuck her —"

Fuck her. Like that's all it had been, something base and somehow shameful, something without meaning. Aside from the very real fact that actually fucking her had been the one thing James had forbidden them, it turned Alex's stomach to think of his time with Anne in that way. *Meaningless.*

"Don't," Alex repeated sharply, his tone far different than it had been even a minute before.

"I shouldn't have told her it was okay to meet you that last time," Jamie persisted, but something in Alex's expression finally stopped him.

Alex couldn't tell Jamie that he loved her. That last day in the Sandusky hotel, Anne had come to him with a purpose and reasons of her own, and Alex had done everything she asked of him except tell her that he would stay.

Jamie had given his permission for it, his blessing, and now he regretted it. But Alex didn't and never could, because he could never wish away that love. He could pray for it to go away, not that he believed in any kind of god that would grant that request, but he could *never* wish that he'd never had it.

"What do you want? Why are you here?" Alex demanded.

Jamie kissed him.

Surprised, Alex opened to the sudden embrace. Jamie's hands moved to the small of Alex's back, pulling him closer. Their mouths opened. Tongues tangled and stroked. Their teeth clashed, jarring. Not their first kiss, but the first in a long, long time, and maybe the last.

When Jamie pulled away, his face was flushed. Alex didn't think he'd been drinking, but he recognized his best friend's expression. That edge of belligerence. It was the same as it had been that night so many years ago, back home in Sandusky. The night before Alex had left for Singapore.

Alex took a step back, his heart aching. He clenched his fists, feeling sweaty palms and twitching fingers. He didn't want to fight Jamie again. Not ever again.

"Don't leave." Jamie said this warningly, although Alex hadn't made so much as a glance toward the door.

"I'm not leaving."

Jamie let out a sigh. "Good. That's good."

Alex wiped his hand over his mouth, still damp from his best friend's kiss. "If you came here to fuck me —"

"No," Jamie interrupted, adding in a lower voice, "I

mean, not only that. No."

"What, then?" Alex asked, wary and hating himself for being disappointed. Going to bed with Jamie would be one more mistake in a long, long line of the ones he'd made, but there'd always been something there between them and always would.

"I miss you, man. I miss talking to you. I miss seeing you. I want you in my life, even if…" Jamie cleared his throat and cut his gaze from Alex. He put his hand on the back of his neck and turned away, going to the window to look out. "Look, we can just forget what happened over the summer. Okay?"

"I can't do that." He would never be able to forget it, any of it.

"Please," Jamie said. "What do I have to do, Alex? I can't stand it, man. You're just fucking…gone."

"I've been gone before."

"Not like this," Jamie said.

Alex went to the bed, a vast king-sized expanse of white sheets and fluffy pillows. He sat on the edge, facing the television set and the desk and the mini-fridge. He put his hands, loosely linked, between his knees. He studied his feet and the carpet, worn in places where the desk chair's wheels had rubbed it free of the geometric pattern.

"We've both fucked up," Jamie said when Alex didn't answer him. "But that doesn't have to mean it's just over, does it? All of the years, our friendship, everything? It can't just be gone. I won't let it be."

Jamie sat next to Alex, their thighs touching. He took Alex's hand. Linked their fingers. Squeezed.

They sat like that for a while, neither speaking. When Jamie shifted to move back on the bed, tugging Alex with him, Alex didn't protest. Everything in the room had gone misty, like in a dream. He shouldn't give in to this. More importantly, he shouldn't let Jamie. Alex would get over this, but Jamie…he'd hold onto it and hate himself when it was over.

"It will change everything," Alex said as they lay on their sides, heads on matching pillows, facing each other. He slid his hand up Jamie's arm to rest on his shoulder. One knee cocked to move between Jamie's. "I can't lose you."

"You're not going to lose me. You could never lose me. I love you." Jamie said this as easily and confidently as he always did. His voice had edged, though, with something sharp and a little broken. "I love you."

They clutched each other. There was more than sex in this embrace, this grasping, desperate gripping by them both. Their bodies pressed together. They kissed, yes, but more than that, they buried their faces against each other's necks. Chests. They burrowed into each other like they were trying to meld.

Alex could feel Jamie's hardness between them. His own cock was stiff. How could it not be? This was Jamie, his best friend, the first person Alex had ever loved. They'd danced around this desire for decades.

The kissing slowed. Their bodies, still pressed together, relaxed. They held onto each other, but the writhing and grinding stopped. Jamie nudged his head into the space between Alex's neck and shoulder and kept it there. His shoulders rose and fell with a series of sighs, and his entire body trembled.

Alex put his arms around Jamie. He kissed the top of his friend's head. They stayed that way long enough for the sun slanting through the window's slatted blinds to moved across the bed.

"I love you," Jamie said against Alex's neck. "I want to do this with you. But not if you don't want to."

Alex traced circles on Jamie's back with a fingertip. "Remember how we used to write out words like this? And try to guess them?"

"Yes."

He traced a heart on Jamie's back. That was cheating a little bit, since it wasn't a letter but a shape. Jamie sighed again. His hand went to Alex's hip and rested there.

"We aren't going to run away together, Jamie. We aren't going to live together, doing this. You think you want this — "

"I do want it!"

"You don't want to take me around to your parents' house and tell them I'm the new Mrs. Kinney. You don't want to explain to your boss why I'm at your side at the company picnic. You don't want to hurt Anne, Jamie. You don't want to lose her or your marriage for anything. Not even this."

Jamie answered after a hesitation. "I know that."

"If we do this, it will change everything."

"Everything changes," Jamie said.

Alex kissed the top of his head again. "I don't want us to change, Jamie. I'm sorry it can't be different. But I don't want us to change who we are to each other. *How* we are."

Sometimes, Alex thought, the words he said in times like this, in these moments of disarray, were the only honest words he ever spoke. He waited for Jamie to argue with him. Maybe, to fight him again. He braced himself for vitriol and fury and disappointment.

Jamie only kissed Alex's throat and squeezed him hard enough to almost hurt. Then he sat up. He swung his legs over the bed, facing away from Alex. His shoulders hunched. Every line of his body broadcast his sorrow, but his voice was steady when he said, "Okay."

Alex pushed himself up against the headboard and

drew his knees in to his chin. He rested his forehead there. He closed his eyes.

"I came here to do whatever it took to make sure we were good again. That's all that matters to me," Jamie said.

Alex looked up to see his friend staring over his shoulder. "I want us to be good again, too."

"Good." Jamie's smile didn't reach his eyes, but it was still a smile.

For one instant, Alex regretted this choice. He wondered if was always going to do that, try to do the right thing and be sorry for it. He could change it. Jamie's face told him that. He could reach for his friend and pull him close. Undress him. Kiss him, suck him, fuck him, come with him.

But he could love Jamie without all that, too. It would last longer and be better for both of them. So instead of giving in to desire, Alex submitted to love, that long-term goal, the best thing and only thing he could offer.

Chapter 14

"Come to Cleveland. See the show with me, like old times. That'll be okay, won't it?" Jamie looked anxious.

They'd slept together in that king-sized bed, their bodies touching. Alex hadn't slept without dreams in so long it felt like he'd drowned. He woke in the darkness to the sound of Jamie in the bathroom. He had a flight to catch, leaving early. He needed to get on the shuttle.

But first, this.

"I'll treat for the tickets, even, how's that?" Jamie added a smile that seemed a little more genuine.

Alex nodded. "Sure, man. That sounds awesome. But I'm not coming back home for a while. You know that, right?"

"Yeah, sure. That's fine. I don't blame you for that." Jamie paused and moved awkwardly to embrace him. He let go too fast.

Yesterday's intimacy had been shoved into the background again, but Alex could hardly be upset, could he?

He'd been the one to make sure of it. Alex took a step back to put even more distance between them.

"Will she be there?" Alex asked.

"Yeah, sure. Of course she will." He'd said it sort of like a challenge or a test, and a little like he expected Alex to fail it. His expression didn't so much as twitch. "Is that cool?"

Alex gave Jamie a long and steady look. "Yeah. It's cool."

They parted ways in the hotel lobby with a handshake. No embrace. What had happened had not ruined them, but it had changed them.

Chapter 15

Jamie had told Alex that Anne was going to be at the concert. Alex hadn't thought to ask him if Jamie had told her. He should have. They'd agreed to meet for dinner and drinks, first. When Alex walked in, it was obvious Anne hadn't expected him to be there.

"Hey, fucker." Jamie stood to greet him.

They hugged, slapping backs, knuckling biceps. Alex thought about kissing Jamie on the cheek, but did not. Everything was still too raw, too new. The memory of Jamie's hard cock against him twisted his insides almost worse than the sight of Anne's face as she saw him for the first time.

She had not known, and if Alex could have turned on his heel and disappeared without her seeing him, he would have. Her eyes lit, burning, then skated away from his like the sight of him made her sick. Her lips pressed into a thin, grim line. Her expression fucking killed him, a slaughter made more painful because he could tell she thought keeping the secret had been his idea. He took the seat across from her, aware of how close their knees were to brushing, even more acutely aware of how they did not.

"First round's on me," Jamie said. "You can pick up the rest of the tab, moneybags."

Alex had not had a drink since before the day he'd met Jamie in that airport hotel room. It had not been a conscious decision, this sobriety, but the longer it went, the better it felt. Facing things without the haze of booze or drugs, or hell, even the afterglow that fucking brought wasn't easy, but he supposed nothing worth doing could be. If he didn't exactly greet every dawn with a war cry, at least he was doing his best to make some changes in his life. Tonight, though, was not a time to be sober.

"Gin Rickey," Alex ordered.

Jamie waggled his hand with his little finger extended. "When in doubt, pinky out. Since when did you get to be such a fancy motherfucker?"

"How many have you had already?" Alex shot back.

Jamie laughed and slung a casual arm around Anne's shoulders. His wife, Alex forced himself to think. To remember. Anne was Jamie's *wife*. "A few."

All through dinner, Alex barely heard a word his old pal Jamie had to say. He was too focused on the way Anne's hands shook when she picked up her silverware. She wouldn't look at him, and all he could do was drink in the sight of her. If yearning was flammable, his would have set the table on fire.

By the time they were ready to head over to the concert, he and Jamie were pretty lit. When they crossed the street from the restaurant to the club, Alex automatically reached for Anne's arm to make sure she didn't stumble. She didn't yank it away. She didn't make a scene. But she pulled away and gave him a disgusted look.

"Hey," he said, stupid and too drunk for this early in

the night, trying to make nice. Wanting desperately for her to not only look at him, but to see him. "It's all good. We're good."

She didn't answer him.

General admission. A surging crowd. The opening act had already gone through half their set by the time the three of them found a spot toward the back, near the thick black-painted pillars that held up the balcony. There was a little more breathing room here, but not much. Alex was too conscious of her presence so close to him.

"Shots," Jamie said with a flick of his fingers toward the bar. "Babe, you want anything?"

Anne shook her head. "I'll stay here."

Jamie linked his arm through Alex's as they headed for the bar. He'd been talking nonstop since they sat down at the restaurant, and he wasn't stopping now. They got in line, and Jamie leaned in to whisper into Alex's ear.

"I'm glad you're here."

Alex bumped Jamie with his hip. The drinks had gone down smooth and easy, the way they almost always did. "Fuck you."

"Fuck you harder," Jamie agreed with a grin.

Jamie leaned in. Alex turned his head to avoid the kiss. This wasn't the kind of place where two dudes could make out, not without fear, but Jamie didn't seem to notice or care. He had a straight man's confidence in his invulnerability and his right to do whatever he wanted, wherever he wanted to do it.

Jamie frowned at the rebuff. "Yeah, fuck you, man."

By that time, they'd reached the bar. Jamie ordered shots of whiskey, because nobody fucking ever did shots of gin, and they both tossed them back with identical grimaces. Jamie's few seconds of anger seemed to fade with the burn of the liquor, and he was back to grinning and blabbing as they ordered plastic cups with other drinks and pushed back through the crowd to find Anne.

The lights came up when the opening act left the stage, and the bass thumping of a recent club hit started pulsing. The crowd wasn't drunk enough to start dancing yet. Anne leaned against the pillar with her arms crossed, watching her husband as he spoke so animatedly that he sloshed his drink over his hand and onto the floor.

"And this fucker," Jamie said abruptly with a grand wave toward Alex, "says he's not coming home again."

Startled but fuzzy from the drinks, Alex knew he ought to have a retort to that, but all he could do was look at Anne to see what she thought of that. The slash of colored lights over her face disturbed him. It looked like blood. Her eyes were vast, deep pools of nothing.

"Why would he?" Anne directed the question at her husband, but her gaze had finally rested on Alex's.

Jamie blathered an answer that neither of them seemed to hear. Alex downed the last of his drink and went to the garbage can to toss it. When he got back, Anne was gone.

"Bathroom," Jamie said, although Alex hadn't asked.

"I never said I wasn't going home again." Alex had to shout over the sudden surge of the music. "I said not for a while! I never said it would be forever!"

Jamie held a hand up to his ear, acting like he couldn't hear what Alex was saying. The lights went down, and there was no more time to talk because the band came on with their trademark thrill of guitars. The lead vocalist kicked a high-heeled boot toward the audience as she launched into the first chords of one of their top hits, *Deadly Kiss of Poison*. Her voice followed a moment later with the lyrics, and the crowd went wild.

Everyone was dancing now. And there in the crowd, Alex found himself next to Anne. Shit. Like it was an accident, except he'd seen her come out of the bathroom and he'd pushed his way through the rest of the people surrounding her to make sure he put himself there.

It would be okay, he told himself. He didn't need to touch her. He could simply be next to her, behind her, near her; he could watch her watching the band and see the lights dancing across her face, and that was all he had to do.

He could love her, and it would all still be okay.

Alex had loved Jamie since they were kids. He'd loved other women, in his own way, although he knew it was doubtful that any of them would've believed they'd ever had anything close to love from him. But Anne, Anne, oh, Anne, it was so different with her and had been from the start. Sex. Lust. Love. Guilt. Everything had become all tangled up inside him, and whatever Alex might have thought about himself, he *knew* for a fact that he was a selfish prick.

He wanted to touch her.

He moved up behind her and slid a hand into the thickness of her hair. He meant to cup the back of her neck, but instead wrapped his fingers in the fall of auburn curls and tugged her back against his body. She moved. She molded herself to him, her ass pressing sweetly and perfectly into his groin. What they did could barely be called dancing, not with the crowd pressing in from all sides preventing any kind of real movement. Jamie was two feet away, bouncing and throwing up the devil horns, mouthing the lyrics. Alex and Anne moved together for a minute or so, and all he could do was soak her in.

Until she turned, that look of disgust back on her face. She put her fingertips on his chest, over his heart, and shoved. Hard. It hurt. Not just the physical touch, her fingers digging into the meat of his chest, but the way she did it so vehemently. She was pissed, but worse, Alex saw the flash of tears in her eyes and the corners of her mouth turning down. She was crying. He'd done that to her. All he'd wanted was to touch her again, even if it could only be for a minute or two or ten, and instead he'd been a colossal asshole and hurt her.

Again.

"You are so beautiful," he said, half-hoping she wouldn't be able to hear him.

"You," she said, and he had no trouble hearing her even over the music and the cacophony of the crowd. "I don't trust you."

There was more drinking after that. Dancing. The band played on. Alex danced with Jamie and by himself, but he gave Anne a wide berth.

When the concert ended and the DJ had stopped spinning, it should have been time to go back to the hotel. Jamie, however, insisted that the three of them stop for pancakes. Two in the morning, and that motherfucker wanted pancakes. Alex didn't want the night to end, and Anne kept her mouth shut on the subject. A whole bunch of other people had the same idea, it seemed, because the place was crowded. They ended up at a tiny table crammed toward the back.

This time, their knees were definitely touching.

Jamie ordered for all of them. Too much food. The pancake place specialized in weird combinations, stacks layered with kids' sugary cereal or candy. Anne picked at hers. Jamie devoured his. Alex took a few bites, hoping he wasn't going to regret this in a few hours.

There'd been music playing the entire time they were there, but in the background. Nothing Alex had paid attention to. At least, not until this song came on. Anne, who'd been smiling at something Jamie said, stopped smiling. Everything else seemed to stop, too.

It wasn't a song she and Alex had ever listened to. Too recent for that. But he'd heard it before. Currently popular on the radio, it was a typical breakup song about lost love, not wanting to go through it again, not going back to the person who hurt you again.

"New room," the vocalist sang. "Same view. Nothing I can do, except stop loving you."

Jamie didn't seem to notice the way Anne turned inward, shrinking away from Alex. Her entire body tensed. She stared into the mug of coffee she'd cupped between her hands. Her expression went blank. Sterile. When she looked at him, Alex realized it was better when she wouldn't. Seeing what he'd done to her was like watching her set herself on fire. He couldn't stop it; all he could do was watch her burn.

The hotel where they'd all booked rooms was also walking distance from the pancake house. On the way back there, Alex was careful to stay on his own side of the sidewalk. He was sobering up a little, but Jamie was pretty trashed. He put his arm around Alex's waist on one side, over Anne's shoulders on the other.

"My favorite people in the whole world. My favorite friend. My favorite wife."

"You're going to be a very sad dude in the morning," Alex told him as the three of them staggered through the lobby and into the elevator.

Twenty minutes after they parted ways to go to their separate rooms, she knocked on his door. He let her in. Of course he did. Some stupid part of him hoped that she was there to fuck or forgive him, and he'd have settled for either.

She wasn't.

"Are you here to ask me to run away with you?" Anne asked in a flat, brittle voice. She was nowhere near close enough for him to touch her, but with the look on her face, even a stupidass prick like Alex Kennedy wouldn't have dared.

"Jamie asked me to the concert." His words were thick, unwieldy, his clumsy tongue making them sound combative when he didn't mean to be.

Anne crossed her arms, a defensive posture. Protecting her heart. Alex wanted to put a hand over his own to push away his own pain.

"I didn't know he didn't tell you I'd be there," Alex said.

"Why *are* you here?" Anne asked.

Words came out, but like a dumbass, they weren't what he really wanted to say. "I thought it would be fun."

He might as well have slapped her in the face, the way she flinched. Anne closed her eyes, turning away. Alex had never felt so small.

"You are so selfish," she whispered. Then again, louder. "Selfish."

He wanted to protest, but she was right.

"You knew how I feel about you, and you show up to a fucking concert? Like nothing happened? Like you didn't fucking break my heart into a million pieces, and what, you just think you can come along and put your hands all over me and make me want you again?"

"Anne…"

But she wasn't having any of it.

"I've tried to hate you, and there are times when I almost make it, Alex. I *almost* hate you. And then I am reminded that I love you, and everything hurts all over again, and I want to hate you but all I can do is hate myself for ever thinking that maybe you had one shred of feeling for me." She held up a hand to stop him from speaking, although all he'd managed was a noise from the depths of his throat. "But obviously, you think nothing of me. You care nothing for me. If you did, if you had the tiniest crumb of love for me, you would never have done this. You would never have been so simply, casually selfish. But that's what I guess I should expect from you, isn't it? It's all you've ever been. It's all you will ever be."

Alex reached for her then, or maybe Anne moved toward him, maybe to hit him, maybe because she wanted this, too, but she was in his arms. She kissed him like she wanted to punch him in the face with her lips. He pulled away bruised and stinging, tasting blood and her tears. It didn't matter if Anne couldn't bring herself to hate him. He hated himself enough for both of them.

"I'm sorry," he said. It wasn't enough. It couldn't ever be enough, but he said it because it was the only thing he could say. "I'm sorry, Anne, I'm really sorry."

She let him hold her. She didn't relax against him at first. It was like hugging a board or a rod of iron. But she pressed her face to the side of his neck after a minute, and her arms went around him.

She whispered in his ear, "I hate you."

That glorious, tragic summer, they'd spent hours in and out of bed, getting each other off, but right then all Alex could think about was the times when she'd fallen asleep next to him. When he'd listened to the sound of her breathing soften and slow and the weight of her relax. He'd been happy next to Anne. Who doesn't want to be happy?

"I'm sorry. If I could take it all back—"

"No. Don't you fucking dare take any of it back." Anne glared. Angry. Sad. Beautiful, so fucking beautiful it ended him. Always and ever his but never belonging to him, his Anne. "Don't you fucking dare."

In the silence that grew between them, all he could think of was how much he wanted to kiss her again. He didn't. Perhaps for the first time, he was man enough not to take what he wanted and say fuck the consequences. She studied him, and Alex had no idea what she was thinking. He guessed he never had.

"Are you here to ask me to run away with you, Alex?" Anne asked again.

He could have said yes, and meant it, at least in that moment. But instead, he gave her the truth that would last a lot longer than a minute. "No."

She nodded and stepped away from him, though she let their fingers link and linger. "Thanks for not lying."

"Would you have said yes?"

Anne laughed. "Oh, Alex."

"That's not an answer."

Her lip curled. She dropped his hand. "Yeah? Well, you don't get a different one. You don't get to come back to me and touch me and ask me questions like that."

"I'm sorry."

"You said that already." She shook her head. Her eyes were bright, but she wasn't crying. "You know, even two or three months ago, I would've said yes. But now…"

"Not now?"

"Not now."

Alex sat on the edge of the bed. It was late. He'd been drunk but now exhaustion overwhelmed him. And he did love her, more than he'd ever known he could love another person.

"I'm sorry, Anne. I really am. For everything. I won't take it back," he said hastily, before she could interrupt. "But fuck, I am so fucking sorry that I hurt you."

He'd never apologized to anyone before that. Not in that way, not meaning it. If getting on his knees for her would've made a difference, believe it, he'd have been there with his face on the grotty hotel carpet. But all he did was sit on the edge of the bed and look at her, hoping she would forgive him even though he didn't deserve it.

"I love you, Alex. But I love my husband, too. And you're his best friend, and I know you love him, and he loves you, and all of this is a huge fucking disastrous mess, but…" She drew in a long, shaky breath. "But when you love someone, you want them to be happy, and I want you to be happy. I want James to be happy. *I* want to be happy."

Anne drew in another breath and looked him in the eyes. "I'm pregnant."

For a crazy, terrifying, amazing few seconds, he thought the kid was his. It had been six months since he'd seen her. If she was six months along, she was hiding it really well.

"I love you, Alex, but I'm *married* to James. We're going to have a baby. I want you to be happy, but I don't want you to ever again touch me the way you did tonight." She paused. "How does that make you feel?"

"Like shit," he answered honestly.

"Good. I hope it breaks you. I hope the thought of never touching me again makes you want to die," Anne said.

It did. She kissed him, then. Softer than the first time. They got into bed together, all their clothes still on, and she fit herself against him. Spooning. He breathed her in and felt her fall asleep next to him. He tried hard to stay awake so he could keep as much of her as he could, but he didn't make it.

When he woke up, she was gone.

Chapter 16

Back to Philly. It wasn't home, but it was the last place Alex had landed, and at least it was a place to stay until he figured his shit out. The Hershey gig was still up for grabs. Alex could stay with Patrick and his husband Teddy in Harrisburg, that had been the offer. Alex wasn't sure he wanted to take the guy up on it — it felt as though there might be some expectations going along with what on the surface seemed to be a generous offer. Still, he appreciated the leads on the work. He might not need the money, but he needed the distraction.

When he closed his eyes, he could still feel and smell and taste Anne Kinney, but she had made it clear there would never be anything more between them, and somehow, that had started to make it easier for him to…well. Not to get over her. He didn't think his love for Anne was ever going to be something he could get "over." But he could move beyond it, leave it behind, move forward. Yeah. He could do that.

He had to do that.

"Welcome back, Mr. Kennedy." The front desk clerk, a

perky blonde with perfect brows and a Marilyn Monroe beauty mark smiled at him. "I have you checking out the day after tomorrow, is that correct?"

Alex returned her smile, but kept it dialed back. He couldn't tell if she was flirting with him or not, and that was a disturbing realization, that he'd lost some of his flirt-meter. "Not sure yet."

She typed rapidly, swiped his credit card, and slid a key across to him. "Have a great day."

Definitely not flirting, then. He took the key and gave her a nod, then went upstairs. He had a new room, but the same view, and if that wasn't the best description for his life, he didn't know what was.

Chapter 17

Alex was not in the mood for dancing, especially not country line dancing, but The Rusty Nail served one of the best bacon cheeseburgers he'd ever had, and it was close enough to his hotel that he could easily walk. This early in the evening he didn't expect there to be much of a crowd, but apparently lot of other hungry carnivores had the same idea. He was seated at a small two-top near what would later clear out to become the dance floor.

The waitress did not flirt with him. If anything, she gave him even less attention than the front desk clerk had. Maybe that grinning cat was right, and they were all fucking mad here. He sure as hell sometimes felt like he'd gone totally insane. He almost wanted to give himself a surreptitious sniff or head for the bathroom to make sure he didn't have something green in his teeth. He settled for digging into his burger and onion rings, savoring every delicious and disgusting bite. His gut was going to hate him for this indulgence, but what the hell. Based on the past couple days, he was headed for a dry spell in his sex life, and that wouldn't be a bad thing.

He needed time, he thought as he dragged an onion ring through some ketchup. The idea was sobering. He'd been on the prowl pretty much since he'd had his first boner. The concept of celibacy had never appealed to him and sure as shit had never been necessary for him in the past. If anything, Alex had been blessed — or cursed, with a surfeit of sexual opportunities. He could take some time off. Find himself, wasn't that what people did after a heartbreak?

Yeah. He'd take some time to find himself. Figure out who he was, what he wanted.

Alex laughed aloud into his beer at that crunchy granola, sandal-wearing bunch of bullshit his brain had conjured. The chuckle hurt him deep in the chest, in the place where his heart was still valiantly beating despite all the damage he'd done to it. He knew who he was. He'd told Anne he was a ragged rascal, and that hadn't changed. Probably never would.

His laughter cut off abruptly when he looked across the bar and saw Luke. He wasn't alone. The girl who'd thrown the engagement ring back at him sat at the same table. They were holding hands across the length of it. Smiling. Laughing. They looked happy.

Well, that was something, wasn't it? And who would Alex be to judge, if Luke had decided to do whatever he had to in order to get his girl to forgive him? It wasn't any of *his* business. The fact that this was the very bar where he'd met Luke in the first place, taken him home, fucked him…it wasn't a sign of anything except that probably he should get out of here before either of them saw him.

He paid his bill and avoided looking in Luke's direction. Alex didn't want any drama. He wanted to finish this gluttonous meal, pay his bill and head home to sleep off the food. No such luck, though, because a shadow fell over the table.

"Luke," Alex said evenly.

"What are you doing here?"

Alex gestured at the plate. "Eating dinner."

Luke glanced over his shoulder toward his table, and Alex followed his gaze. The young woman wasn't there. Maybe she'd gone to the bathroom. Luke turned back, pitching his voice low.

"I didn't know you were still in town."

"There's no reason for you to know," Alex said.

Luke frowned. "I want to see you. Tonight. I'll drop her off —"

"That's not a good idea," Alex interrupted, keeping his voice light. Non-confrontational. "I'm sure you know that, man."

"I have to," Luke said. "Please."

Alex drew in a deep breath and closed his eyes for a second. When he opened them, Luke was still there. "Fine. I'm at the same hotel. Room 510. Come by whenever."

Luke nodded stiffly and headed back to the table, slipping into his seat before his girlfriend or fiancée or whatever she was got back. Alex had no more appetite for his meal. He gestured for the check. Paid it. Left The Rusty Nail without so much as a glance at Luke.

The walk back to the hotel didn't take long, but it was enough time for Alex to consider checking out of the hotel and making his escape before Luke could get there. Hell, he could even leave his baggage behind. There was nothing he didn't have the money to replace. This, the idea of a fresh start, was so appealing that he was already calculating where he'd go. Back in his room, though, there was that view again.

A new room but the same view.

He wasn't going to run away this time. Whatever Luke had to say to him, Alex would hear. Even if it was painful.

The night dragged on so long that Alex stopped expecting a knock on the door. He'd showered and put on his pair of faded Batman pajama bottoms. Played around on his laptop for a while, following up on some consulting projects. It was the earliest he'd been in bed — alone and sober, anyway, in so long he couldn't remember the last time. He'd just turned off the light when the rap came at the door.

Alex braced himself for Luke to be drunk. Maybe he'd even have the girlfriend in tow. He opened the door to find the other guy alone, and if he'd been drinking, he wasn't showing signs of it.

"Hi," Luke said.

Alex stepped aside to let him in. Closed the door behind him. Turned. "Hi."

Luke sat on the edge of the bed without being invited. He linked his fingers together, holding his hands in his lap. He cleared his throat, but didn't speak.

Alex sat in the desk chair, twirling it to face Luke. "What's up?"

"I wasn't expecting to see you there tonight."

"I wasn't expecting you, either," Alex said, then added, "is everything cool?"

Luke nodded. Then shook his head. "No. Shit. I don't know. I thought….shit, man. I don't know."

"You looked pretty happy," Alex said.

Luke grimaced. "She's happy. She said she's willing to forget she ever saw anything. She's not going to tell anyone."

"If you think that's true, then you're kind of a sucker," Alex told him, but kindly.

"She promised."

Alex shrugged. "People make promises they can't keep, man. Your girl…if she didn't tell at least one good girl friend or her sister or her mom or somebody as soon as she found us, you can believe that she will the first time you piss her off."

"She's not like that." Luke had said that before, but now he sounded uncertain.

"Everyone is like that," Alex said.

Luke sighed and ran his hands through the cropped bristle of his hair. He got up, started pacing, stopped himself short. He turned toward Alex.

"I don't want to lose my family. Or my friends. How'd you deal with it?"

Alex shrugged again. "I lost my family. Some friends. You learn to deal with it."

"Shit. I don't want to learn to deal with it," Luke muttered. He sat again on the edge of the bed. His leg jittered up and down, fast, until Alex reached to put a hand on it to stop him. Luke calmed, but barely.

"You're the only person who can decide what's best for you. But let me give you some advice, since you seem to think I'm the guy with the answers. If you don't want to be with her — "

"I love her!" Luke sounded agonized.

Alex could relate.

"You can love her all you want, hell, even if you don't want," Alex snapped. "But if you don't want to *be with* her, let her go. Better to hurt her once, even twice, than over and over again. Because you will, man. Eventually, you will break her. And that probably will break you. "

Luke made a strangled, desperate noise. "How do I know what I fucking want?"

"How does anybody know? I have no idea. Maybe you're meant to get married, have babies and the house with the white picket fence and a big old pickup truck. But if you have thoughts at all that you might be the guy to tell his wife he's going bowling and instead sneaks off to get his dick sucked by a stranger he picks up in a gay bar, you'd better be sure you're ok with being that guy. And shit, Luke…even I can see you're not that kind of guy." Alex shook his head. "You're a good guy. A *nice* guy."

"You don't make that sound like a compliment." Luke sounded and looked miserable.

"It's not an insult." Alex moved from the chair to the bed. He took Luke's hand as they sat shoulder-to-shoulder. "I meant you're not an asshole, like me."

"You're not an asshole." At the sight of Alex's expression, Luke laughed and amended, "Okay, so you're not a total asshole. You have a few redeeming qualities."

Alex nudged him with his shoulder. "Don't tell me what they are. I'll get a swelled head."

Luke sighed and half-turned to put his forehead on Alex's shoulder. "I thought seeing you tonight meant something. Like the universe was telling me what to do. But now that I'm here with you, I still don't know."

Alex stroked his hand over the back of Luke's head. "You don't have to decide right this second what to do for the rest of your life. You can just figure out what you need to do for tonight. Then tomorrow. Then the day after that. But you do have to decide, man."

"What if what I want to do tonight is you?" Luke whispered.

Alex didn't move away. He tipped his head to press his lips to the other man's forehead. He'd already made so many mistakes, some of them with Luke. He was going to try his best not to keep making them.

"Sometimes, not getting what you want is better in the long run," Alex said.

Luke laughed bitterly and sat back. His eyes glittered with unshed tears. Two spots of bright color painted his cheeks.

"You sound like you know what you're talking about."

"I never know what I'm talking about," Alex told him. "I'm a bullshitter, and I lie. All the time."

Luke shook his head. "You're not lying."

"Not right now. No."

"If I asked you, right now, to tell me that you wanted to be with me. Like try a real thing. What would you say?"

Alex chose his answer carefully. "I can't say that."

"Lie, then," Luke said. "You lie all the time, so lie about this!"

Alex shook his head in silence. Luke's shoulders slumped. He pulled his hand from Alex's grip and used his other one to rub it, as though the touch had left a bruise.

"I'm not the guy you want for real. I'm the guy you fuck because you're curious. I'm the one you fuck because you're lonely. Or confused. I'm just the guy you fuck," Alex said. "That's all."

Luke got to his feet, staggering once but catching himself before he could stumble. It was the first time he'd seemed less than sober tonight, but Alex knew Luke wasn't drunk. Something inside him was cracking, getting ready to shatter.

"That's not all you are," Luke said.

Alex stood, too. "That's all I am for you. It's all I'll ever be able to be."

Luke pulled himself up straight. Squared his shoulders. Lifted his chin.

"I'll be fine," he said. "I'll figure it out."

"Yeah, absolutely. You will."

At the door, Luke turned. "It would have been better if you'd been able to lie to me, at least for an hour or two."

He didn't wait for Alex to answer him. Alex locked the door behind him, one hand on it, then put his forehead to it as he closed his eyes and listened to the sound of Luke on the other side. He still had the chance, this one last chance, to open up the door, but he knew that no matter what Luke thought, it would not have been better for either of them if Alex had lied.

Chapter 18

Alex had enough friends in enough places that all he needed was a plane ticket and an overnight bag. He had both within a few hours. He slept on the plane. He got off the plane. He got a cab to a friend's house. Madeline was an acquaintance of a generous nature, with a nice guest room and low expectations. She'd been through a recent divorce and was not interested in dating or even fucking.

"That's the only reason I let you stay here," she told Alex over mugs of hot, sweet tea and a plate of scones. "Because believe me, if I was in the mood to get laid, I'd have been all over you."

He laughed, but the comment stung. "I appreciate the honesty."

"Always." She studied him over the rim of her cup. "You look different."

The last time he'd seen her had been at the party of a mutual friend. She'd just separated from her husband. "You do, too. You look happy."

"I *am* happy. Ecstatically." Madeline tilted her head,

looking him over with a furrow of her brow. "You don't look happy, Alex."

"I'm not happy."

Madeline reached across the table to take his hand in hers. Alex drew in a breath that became a sigh, a muttering whisper. A small, helpless groan. Her simple kindness had unravelled him.

"When you want to talk about it, I'm here," she said.

He didn't think he would ever *want* to talk about it, but he found himself unable to stop himself from talking about it. The tea went cold, the scones uneaten, while Alex talked. They moved to the living room with glasses of wine, and Alex talked. The next morning, over the breakfast he insisted on cooking for her as a thank-you for the hospitality, Alex talked.

For days. Weeks. A month. And another. Alex told Madeline everything, all about his friendship with Jamie. What had happened with Anne. With Luke. With everyone else in his life he'd ever done wrong or been done wrong by.

When she asked him to travel with her — using her recent ex-husband's money without qualms and more than a little bit of venom, Alex said yes. It was good to have a companion, Madeline told him. Better and safer, in some of the places she wanted to visit, if she had a man at her side. They moved from city to city, country to country, eating and drinking and talking their way around the world.

It took a little over a year.

By the end of it, Madeline had started giving interested glances at the handsome and usually younger men who'd been giving her the eye. "I'm not kicking you out or anything. You know you're welcome to stay as long as you like."

They'd been sipping cocktails in her garden. Most of the flowers had died, but the day had been mild enough for them both to crave the sunshine that the winter would soon chase away. Alex savored the drink before answering.

"I have a friend in the States who's been after me to take on some work in his area."

"A friend," Madeline said with amusement.

Alex laughed. "He's only a friend, as far as I'm concerned."

"With you, I know how that goes." She gave him a small smile. "Will you be all right?"

"If you mean can I resist him? Yeah. Probably. It wouldn't be the first time I disappointed someone who wanted to get me into bed. One of the few times, but not the first," Alex added with a wry laugh. "But I think it's time I move on. Give you some room around here. You can't really get your groove on with me hanging around."

"I could if I wanted to. You've never been a hindrance to that." Madeline flicked her fingertips in his direction and tipped her head back to laugh toward the autumn sky. She looked back at him. "I think I'm ready to at least see what might happen. Thank you for that."

Alex's brows rose. "Me? I haven't done anything. I mean, you're the one who's been holding my hand for the past year or so, listening to me droning on and on about the same thing, over and over. Getting me through. I owe you."

"You gave me someone to love without expectation. I needed that," she told him seriously. "Someone to take care of for a bit, so I'd stop thinking so much about how much I needed taken care of."

He wasn't ashamed to cry in front of her. They'd gone past that, long ago. Alex swiped at his eyes, throat closing with emotion.

"I've been happy to take care of you," he said.

Madeline smiled and brushed the fall of her silver hair out of her eyes. "But you're not happy, Alex."

That was true. The best he could say was that he was at least no longer relentlessly miserable. "Maybe one day."

"One day, indeed. Let's hope it's sooner than you think," Madeline agreed.

She took his hand. He kissed the back of it. They sat that way in the garden, enjoying the sun, neither of them speaking about anything at all.

Chapter 19

A small city tucked into the rural countryside, Harrisburg was charming in its way. It had a beautiful capital building and a struggling downtown that had been revitalized more than once but had never managed to stay vital. Patrick lived in a nice little house that had been renovated without losing any of its vintage appeal. He offered Alex a room, but being a permanent house guest for the past year or so had left Alex wanting a little more privacy. A hotel room would lose its appeal quickly, he knew that, but for the time being it felt right.

Patrick, as it turned out, had a lot of single, curious, confused or lonely friends, and many of them were happy to think of Alex as the guy they wanted to fuck. Alex, for all his determination to get his shit together, had never been any good at celibacy. Living with Madeline had made it easier when she held him accountable, but he was back on his own and randy as hell. Patrick's friend Evan made it quickly clear he was down for some rumpy pumpy action to help him get over a recent breakup. It was supposed to be "just for fun." The "fun" lasted all of two weeks, when

Evan made the offhand comment that the extra toothbrushes were in the closet.

Nobody would ever say Alex Kennedy wasn't smart, but sometimes, he sure was a fucking dumbass.

He'd only been keeping a small overnight bag at Evan's house to save him time and effort the few nights he'd stayed over. He didn't want to bother picking it up, counting the loss of some deodorant and a couple of pairs of briefs as collateral damage. He did man up and tell Evan he wasn't going to be coming back around. The fun had ended.

"Just come by and get your things," Evan said. "No drama."

But of course there was drama. There were accusations. There was pleading. There was the throwing of shoes and stamping of feet. Alex had extricated himself as well as he could, knowing he'd gotten what he deserved. One day he'd learn his fucking lesson.

He should've known, though, that Evan would be at Patrick's holiday party.

It was wrong, of course, to go with Evan outside to Patrick's very cold, very cluttered, screened porch, but the offer of a good old fashioned dicksucking had led Alex to a lot of bad decisions in the past. Why should this time be any different? Other than the audience, he thought, as he caught sight of the woman standing in the shadows, mostly hidden by the piles of Patrick's hoarded junk. Alex had been watching her all night, careful to make sure she didn't catch him staring. She was gorgeous — dark hair in braids all over her head, bronze skin, lush mouth and figure.

He should have talked to her, he thought, distracted and still a little high, even as Evan grew himself a wild hair and shoved Alex against the wall like he was trying to be the daddy. Alex turned his face toward the light. If he'd talked to her earlier, maybe he wouldn't be here with Evan, now. He could just barely glimpse her, standing still as a wild deer trying not to catch the attention of a wolf. If he called out to her, would she run?

If she ran, would he want to chase her?

Before Alex had the chance to say anything or think about his silent observer any longer, Evan dropped to his knees and unzipped the front of Alex's trousers. Alex had to shake his hair out of his eyes to look at the man in front of him, so eager to get to Alex's cock that his mouth already gaped. His lips glistened in the dim shaft of light from the yard, making Evan's eagerness not sexy, but somehow unsettling. Like, getting your knob gobbled was one thing, but something about how Evan was acting seemed more like he meant to actually eat Alex's dick. Something like a conscience poked him, which was a fucking joke, because Alex usually ignored the angel on his shoulder, that annoying little fuck.

Still, right now, in the dark and cold and the party still thumping inside, and especially with the woman watching them, Alex had the sense to know that all of this was going to end up going sour in the long run. Hell, in the short run, as in about ten minutes from now when he was done coming down the back of Evan's throat and the poor guy thought that meant a reconciliation. Alex had already gone through drama with Evan. The guy was lovestruck, or something stupid like that.

So, Alex tried. "Evan, you don't have to do this."

"Shut up."

The light from the streetlamp down the alley was barely bright enough to illuminate anything, but it was enough to show Alex what was going on. He didn't dare look toward the corner to see if the woman was still watching. He hadn't seen even the glimmer of movement, so he thought she must be. Watching…and enjoying it? He hoped so. Something about the idea of that was super hot, hot enough that he ignored the danger bells clanging inside him about getting involved again with Evan's crazy.

Evan yanked Alex's trousers down past his knees. Alex had been nursing a semi since they got out onto the porch, but Evan didn't settle for that. He gripped Alex's cock and stroked, stroked, and say what you wanted about the guy being a pretentious asshole, he did know how to get a cock hard. Alex's head tipped back with a dull thud against the wall as the warmth of pleasure washed through him.

"Shut up and take it," Evan said.

Maybe he meant to be menacing or sexy, but Alex only laughed and put his hand on Evan's head to twist and twine his fingers in the other man's hair. Alex jerked Evan's head back seconds before he could get his mouth on Alex's dick.

"Are you fucking serious?" Alex said around his laughter. He loosened his grip enough to let Evan's head bob forward. Evan was, indeed, serious.

There came the soft, wet noise of a mouth on flesh.

"Fuck, that's good," Alex said.

"I know how you like it," Evan said, softer this time, without the attitude.

"Who doesn't?" Alex laughed, low and slow and a little drowsy.

More soft, wet sounds. Alex looked down at Evan and saw the gleam of Evan's smile as he pulled away from Alex's cock. Alex put his hand on Evan's head again. Evan got back to the business of cocksucking.

Alex moaned. Evan made a muffled noise and drew Alex's cock in nice and deep, so that it nudged the back of his throat. His palm cupped Alex's balls and he stroked his thumb along that sweet spot, finding the place to press, just right. Evan could be clinging and jealous and held far too high an opinion of himself. He'd tried too hard, demanded too much from Alex even though he'd made it clear from the start that everything was only casual between them. But fuck, if the guy couldn't suck cock.

The soft, feminine sigh from the corner told him she was still watching, and that was what pushed him over the edge more than the steady stroking of Evan's tongue or the tickle on his balls. She sounded like she might just be getting a little bit herself. Alex arched, hitting his head with a dull thump on the wall.

He was coming, oh fuck yes. Oh, God. He looked for her then, staring deep into the shadows to find her face. Her eyes were closed, her face turned. She wasn't looking at him, and the disappointment softened his cock faster than it otherwise would have.

While Alex had lost his attention to the silent woman in the corner, Evan had gotten to his feet and was aiming his mouth at Alex's. He almost got it there, too, because of the distraction. Alex could smell himself on Evan's breath, a thick ocean scent that normally didn't offend him, but now pissed him off.

"No," Alex said and put his hand up to keep Evan from kissing him. There was distance between them, a space of light in the dark of their two shadows. Evan moved forward again, a little, and Alex stepped to the side.

"No?" Evan mimicked, sounding exactly like the whiny, clingy lover he'd always been. A reminder of exactly why this had been a bad idea. "You'll let me suck your dick, but you won't kiss me?"

Zip. Sigh. Alex shrugged.

"You're a fucking asshole, you know that?"

"I know it," Alex said. "But so did you before you brought me out here."

Evan stamped his foot. Tossing a tantrum. It probably worked on other guys, but it never had on Alex. "I hate you!"

"No, you don't."

"I do!" Evan opened the door to the house and turned back to add dramatically, "You can just forget about coming home!"

Alex rolled his eyes. Yes, it was true. He was an asshole. But he'd been an honest one, at least, and it wasn't his fault Evan had thought he could somehow get around that.

"Your place isn't home. Why do you think I took all my stuff?"

"I fucking hate you. I never should've given you a second chance!" Evan's voice cracked.

For a second, a tiny one, Alex felt a little pity for the other man, who'd once told Alex he was afraid everyone left him because they thought he was unlovable. They'd been in bed, the lights out, both too high even to fuck. Alex had kissed Evan's forehead and told him not to worry so much about what other people thought.

"I told you not to," Alex said.

Evan swept out. Alex stayed behind for another minute or two, his breathing heavy. He wanted to call out to the woman, to ask her what she thought about it. Was he an asshole, he wanted to know. Did he deserve Evan's hatred?

He wanted to ask her, his sexy voyeur, if she thought he, Alex, was unlovable.

But of course, she wouldn't be able to answer him. She didn't know him, and she probably never would. So instead of calling her out to let her know he'd seen her watching, embarrassing them both, causing more drama he didn't need, for once Alex listened to the sane little angel on his shoulder.

He went inside.

Chapter 20

Alex had been looking for his mystery woman all night, but although the party had thinned out a lot, he hadn't found her. She must have gone home. Drunk and weeping, Evan had begged Alex to reconsider, "just one more time."

"Listen to me," Alex said under his breath so that Evan's friends, who were hovering around ready to rescue him from the Big Bad Wolf wouldn't hear. "You are not unlovable. Okay? You're not fucking unlovable, Evan."

"Then why?"

Alex sighed. He put a hand on each of Evan's shoulders. He looked into the other guy's eyes.

"Because I don't want to. Sometimes, that's the only reason."

"Come home with me anyway," Evan said.

Evan's friends pulled him away before Alex could answer, although he had no intentions of taking the other guy up on the offer. Anyway, Patrick had convinced him to stay here, at least for the night. Longer, if he wanted to.

The bedroom they'd given him was small. Barely big

enough for a twin bed with a plush mattress and a small dresser, into which he had not bothered to unpack his duffel bag. He liked sleeping naked, but it was too damned cold in here, so he pulled out the first pair of soft pajama bottoms he could find. They were the Hello Kitty pair he ought to have thrown out long ago, and after he tugged them on, he sat on the bed with his head in hands for a long time.

The pajamas made him think of Anne, which made him think of Jamie, and dammit, wouldn't it have been the perfect hour of the night to call the number of the house on the lake and talk to one or both of them? To ask them if he could come…home, Alex thought, and clapped a hand over his mouth to stop the small cry from leaking out. Anne and Jamie's house could never again be his home. He'd ruined that the summer he'd stayed there, and if it had been salvageable, he'd ruined it again for good after what had happened later. After seeing Anne in Cleveland, Alex knew there was no way he could ever take that sort of advantage again.

"I hope the thought of never touching me again makes you want to die," Anne had told him that night, but he would die rather than hurt her again. Of all the things in his life he'd fucked up, he would never forgive himself for what he'd done to Anne Kinney. Even if she forgave him for it.

A year of talking to Madeline had helped, but it hadn't taken away everything. He would always love Anne Kinney in some small, dark and secret region of his heart. Even if he'd managed to move forward, she would always be in his past.

On his back, beneath the weight of blankets warm enough to keep the room's chill from making him shiver, Alex stared up into the dark and tried to sleep. He should have found it easily enough — booze, weed, food, a blowjob. It ought to have been the perfect prescription for collapsing into dreams, but instead he found himself thinking again of the watching woman.

What had she been doing out there on the porch? A slow surge of arousal filtered through him, remembering Evan's grasping hands and wet mouth on his cock, knowing she'd been watching them without saying a word.

For a second, Alex hated his betraying cock for always being ready. Hated himself for always using sex as a way to forget what a bastard he was. A rascal, he'd called himself to Anne. It seemed forever ago, their summer by the water.

The memory sent another raw wave of arousal through him. He had stopped thinking of her all the time. He didn't want to be thinking of her now. He rolled onto his belly to bury his face in the pillow and slid his hand into the Hello Kitty pajama bottoms. He gripped his cock. A few strokes and he could sleep.

Again, he thought of the mystery woman. He pictured that lush mouth. Her dark eyes. That fall of gorgeous black hair, styled in the myriad of braids. His cock got thicker.

But after a moment or so, he rolled onto his back again and took his hand away, almost like a punishment. He'd gotten off hard earlier, more from knowing the mystery woman was watching than from Evan's overeager and sort of sloppy beej. That had seemed fine at the time, or at the very least, it had felt like she was a willing participant.

This, though…fuck. He groaned and writhed for a moment in the bed, fisting both his hands in his hair and pumping his hips against the covers before going still. This was using her to push away bad memories. She'd never know about it. He was unlikely to ever even see her again. Even so, he couldn't do it.

He might be an arrogant bastard, a rascal, a rogue; he

was definitely an asshole. But just then, Alex decided that he was done being the guy who used other people, with or without their consent. With or without their knowledge.

At three in the morning, epiphanies always seem profound, but in the light of morning will fade. When Alex woke, however, far earlier than he'd expected to, he still felt the same way. He was done. Finished. Kaput. Turning over a new leaf, yadda yadda yadda. The gods of hangover relief must have taken this decision as an offering, because despite last night's indulgences and the too-few hours of sleep, Alex had never felt better.

At least until he headed downstairs to Patrick and Teddy's kitchen, meaning to stuff his face with some breakfast. He pulled up short at the sight of a distinctly female backside protruding from the fridge — but not short enough, because she turned so fast that she almost ran into him.

It was the woman from last night.

Her container of pot-stickers hit the floor and bounced. She screamed. Loud. Taken aback, stunned, but now totally sure that the gods of something or other were definitely smiling down on him, Alex smiled.

"Damn you're pretty," she said so matter-of-factly he couldn't be sure she'd meant it as a compliment.

He blinked, his smile getting wider. He crossed his arms over his naked stomach. "Thanks."

Alex looked at the container by his toes, then at her. He bent to pick it up, but slowly, a thrum of tension building inside him at the idea of being at her feet. It would be a good place for him, he thought.

"Thanks." She took the container and eased past him to put it in the microwave. She looked over her shoulder. "Want some?"

He laughed and shook his head and took a step back.

Uncomfortable. Last night it had been hot to know she'd been watching him get off, but now, in the light of morning…shit, he wished he was wearing a shirt, at least. Things were certainly changing for him, if he could feel embarrassed.

"I'm Olivia," she said.

Her name was Olivia, and she was going to change his life.

Afterword

This novella takes place after Tempted and Everything Changes but before Naked. It includes an alternate version of the events Alex talks about in Vanilla.

Tempted

I had everything a woman could want...

My husband, James. The house on the lake. Our perfect life. And then Alex came to visit. The first time I saw my husband's best friend, I didn't like him. Didn't like how James changed when he was around, didn't like how his penetrating eyes followed me everywhere. But that didn't stop me from wanting him. And, surprisingly, James didn't seem to mind.

It was meant to be fun. Something the three of us shared for those hot summer weeks Alex stayed with us. Nobody was supposed to fall in or out of love. I didn't need another man, not even one who oozed sex like honey and knew all the secrets I didn't know, the secrets my husband hadn't shared. After all, we had a perfect life. And I loved my husband.

But I wasn't the only one.

Excerpt:

The telephone's jangling interrupted the post-coital laziness to which we'd succumbed. The Sunday edition of the Sandusky Register, spread out on the bed, crinkled and rustled as James leaned over me to grab up the phone from its cradle. I took the chance to lick his skin as he did, sneaking a nibble that made him jump and laugh as he answered.

"This better be good," he said into the phone.

A pause. I gave him a curious look over the Lifestyles section. He was grinning.

"You son of a bitch!" James settled back against the headboard, his naked knees pulled up. "What are you doing? Where the hell are you?"

I tried catching his eye but the conversation had immersed him. James is an intense butterfly, flitting from focus to focus and giving each his undivided attention. It's flattering when it's you. Not so charming when it isn't.

"You lucky son of a bitch." James sounded almost envious, and my curiosity was piqued even more. Generally, James was the object of admiration amongst his peers, the one with the newest toys. "I thought you were in Singapore?"

I knew, then, who disrupted our Sunday afternoon lassitude. It had to be Alex Kennedy. I looked back to my paper, listening while James talked. There wasn't anything particularly interesting in the newspaper. I didn't really care about the latest summer fashion or what cars were trendy this year. I cared even less about burglaries and politics, however, so I scanned the columns of text and discovered I'd been ahead of my time in painting my bedroom pale melon the year before. Apparently it was the hot new color for the season.

Listening to only one side of a conversation is like putting together a puzzle without looking at the picture on the box. I listened to James talking to his best friend from junior high school with only the barest comprehension and frame of reference to help me put the pieces together. I knew my husband as well and intimately as any one person can know another, but I didn't know Alex at all.

"Yeah, yeah. Of course you did. You always do."

The keen admiration was back, along with an eagerness new to me. I glanced at James. His face was alight with glee and something else. Something almost poignant. Despite having what could be a somewhat narrow focus on his own priorities, James was unafraid to be happy for someone else's fortune. He was, however, rarely impressed. Or intimidated. Now, he looked a bit of both, and I forgot about the vapidity of pale melon altogether to listen to him speak.

"Ah, get out, man, you'd rule the fucking world if you wanted."

I blinked. The sincere, almost puppyish tone was as new to me as the look on his face. This was startling. A bit disturbing. It was the way a boy speaks to a woman he's convinced he loves even though he knows she'll never give him a second look.

"Yeah, same here." Laughter, low and somewhat secret, crept out of him. Not his usual guffaw. "Fucking-A man, that's great. I'm glad to hear it."

Another pause while he listened. I watched him rub the curving white scar just above his heart. His fingers traced the line of it, over and over, absently. I'd seen him do that before, rubbing that scar like a talisman when he was tired or upset or excited. Sometimes it was brief, a passing touch like he was flicking a crumb from his shirt. Other times, like this, the stroke-stroke of his fingers took on an almost hypnotic pace. I could be mesmerized watching James run his fingers along that scar, which sometimes looks like the half-moon or a bite, or a frown, or a rainbow.

James' brow creased. "No. Really? What were they thinking? That sucks, Alex. Really fucking sucks. Fuck, man, I'm sorry."

From elation to sorrow in half a second. This too was unusual from my husband, who might move easily from focus to focus but always managed to maintain his stability. His syntax had changed during his conversation, reverting a little. I'm no prude about bad language, but he was saying "fuck" an awful lot.

In the next instant, his face brightened. He sat up, bent knees going straight. The sunshine of his smile burst from behind the storm clouds of a moment before.

"Yeah! Right on! Fucking-A! You got it, man! That's fan-fucking-tastic!"

At this I could no longer hide my expression of surprise, but James didn't notice. He was bouncing a little, shaking the bed so the papers rattled and the sadly neglected Classifieds section fluttered to the floor.

"When? Great! That's…yeah, yeah…of course. It'll be fine. It'll be great. Of course I'm sure!" His glance flicked toward me, but I was certain he didn't actually see me. His mind was too taken up with whatever was happening in Singapore. "Can't wait! Yeah. Just let me know. Bye, man. See you."

With that, he thumbed the disconnect button and settled back against the headboard with a grin so broad and vibrant it looked a bit maniacal. I waited for him to speak, to share with me the piece of brilliant news that had so excited him. I waited quite a bit longer than I expected to.

Just as I was about to ask, James turned to me. He kissed me, hard, his fingers tangling in my hair. His mouth bruised mine a little, and I winced.

"Guess what?" He answered before I had time to reply. "Alex's company just got bought out by a much larger corporation. He's like, a fucking millionaire now."

What I knew of Alex Kennedy could have fit on one side of a sheet of notebook paper. I knew he worked overseas in the Asian market and had since before I'd met James. He'd been unable to attend our wedding but had sent an elegant gift that must have been exorbitantly expensive. I knew he'd been James' best friend since the eighth grade, and that they'd had a falling out when they were both twenty-one. I'd always had the feeling the rift had never fully been repaired, but then, men's relationships are so different from women's. If James barely spoke to his friend, that didn't mean they hadn't forgiven each other for whatever it was that had driven them apart.

"Wow. Really? A millionaire?"

James shrugged, fingers tightening again in my hair

before he sat back against the headboard again. "The guy's a fucking genius, Anne. You don't even know."

I didn't know. "That's good news, then. For him."

He frowned, running a hand through dark hair already tipped blond though the summer had barely begun. "Yeah, but the bastards who bought him out have decided they don't want him part of the company any longer. He's out of a job."

"Does a millionaire need to work?"

James gave me a look that said I clearly didn't get it. "Just because you don't have to do something doesn't mean you don't want to. Anyway, Alex is done with Singapore. He's coming home."

His voice trailed off at the last, sounding almost wistful for the barest second before he looked at me with another grin. "I invited him for a visit. He said he'll probably stay for a few weeks while he puts together his next business."

"A few weeks? Here?" I didn't mean to sound unwelcoming, but….

"Yeah." James' grin was small and secret, for himself. "It'll be great. You'll love Alex, babe. I know you will."

He looked at me and was, for an instant, a man I didn't know. He reached for my hand, linking our fingers before he took it to his lips and kissed the back of it. His mouth caressed my skin, and he looked up at me over the top of his kiss, his blue eyes dark with excitement.

But not for me.

Also by Megan Hart

All the Lies We Tell

All the Secrets We Keep

A Heart Full of Stars

Always You

Broken

Castle in the Sand

Clearwater

Crossing the Line

Deeper

Dirty

Don't Deny Me

Everything Changes

Every Part of You

Flying

Hold Me Close

Indecent Experiment

Lovely Wild

Naked

Out of the Dark

Passion Model

Precious and Fragile Things

Reawakened Passions

Ride with the Devil

Selfish is the Heart

Stranger

Stumble into Love

Switch

Tear You Apart

Tempted

The Darkest Embrace

The Favor

The Resurrected: Compendium

The Space Between Us

Vanilla

About the Author

I was born and then I lived awhile. Then I did some stuff and other things. Now, I mostly write books. Some of them use a lot of bad words, but most of the other words are okay.

I can't live without music, the internet, or the ocean, but I have kicked the Coke Zero habit. I can't stand the feeling of corduroy or velvet, and modern art leaves me cold. I write a little bit of everything from horror to romance, and I don't answer to the name "Meg."

Megan Hart is a USA Today, Publisher's Weekly and New York Times bestselling author who writes in many genres including mainstream fiction, erotic fiction, science fiction, romance, fantasy and horror. If you liked this book, please tell everyone you love to buy it. If you hated it, please tell everyone you hate to buy it.

Find me here!
www.meganhart.com
readinbed@gmail.com

facebook.com/READINBED

twitter.com/Megan_Hart

instagram.com/readinbed

bookbub.com/authors/megan-hart

goodreads.com/Megan_Hart

Made in the USA
Middletown, DE
06 January 2019